THE KRYPTEIA

THE KRYPTEIA

A Memoir

ARISTARCHUS

Osiris Mandarin Press

THE KRYPTEIA: A Memoir

Copyright © 2025 by Aristarchus

Content Warning: This book contains graphic depictions of violence, child abuse, cannibalism, suicide, and systematic dehumanization. Reader discretion is strongly advised.

First Edition 2025

ISBN: 979-8-9910882-8-2 (PRINT)

Cover design by JNB

For Kyrillos, who hanged himself

rather than become what I became.

He chose better.

The strong do what they can and the weak suffer what they must.

— THUCYDIDES

CONTENTS

TRANSLATOR'S NOTE

This text has been rendered from Aristarchus's original Greek into contemporary English. Where he used terms specific to ancient medical, military, or technical knowledge, I have mapped these to their modern equivalents so current readers can understand the precise anatomical and tactical concepts he described.

For instance, when Aristarchus writes of specific nerve clusters, pressure points, or anatomical structures, he used Greek terminology that would be opaque to modern readers. Rather than preserve these terms and burden the text with explanations, I have translated his meaning into current medical vocabulary. The same applies to descriptions of psychological states, tactical concepts, and technical processes.

The brutality you read is his. The words through which you comprehend it are mine. But make no mistake—I have softened nothing. Where he wrote of boys eating their dead brothers' fingers, where he catalogued the exact sound a windpipe makes when crushed by hemp rope, where he described watching his blood-brother rehearse his own suicide for two years—all of this comes through exactly as he intended.

I have resisted every modern impulse to soften, contextualize, or redeem. There is no moment where Aristarchus realizes the horror of what he's become. No therapeutic breakthrough. No deathbed conversion. He ends the memoir counting his profits from democratic blood, perfectly content with the weapon he was forged into.

Modern readers desperately want to project their ethics backwards, to find some universal human conscience that transcends time. They want ancient people to be just like us, only wearing different clothes. This is a lie we tell ourselves to avoid confronting the truth: that humans have been capable of creating and becoming monsters without any of the psychological damage we insist must accompany such transformation.

Aristarchus felt no guilt because guilt was never installed in him. The compound didn't break him—it assembled him correctly according to specifications. He's not a modern man struggling with ancient brutality. He's an ancient weapon describing its function with the same detachment a sword would describe cutting.

That total incommensurability—the inability to map modern conscience onto ancient reality—is what makes this document genuine. And it's why modern publishers would never touch it. Not because of the violence, but because it offers no comforting lie that humans have always been essentially the same, that conscience is universal, that people who do horrible things must suffer for it psychologically.

Some truths are too brutal for modern consumption. This is one of them.

A NOTE ON NAMES

Multiple characters share names like Alexios, Nikias, and Dimitri—as common then as Michael or John today. These aren't the same people, just common names accumulating through the violence. That the narrator ultimately assumes "Nikias" for his cover identity is either the compound's final lesson in emptying oneself, or something worse—wearing the name of his victims like a burial shroud worn inside out.

THE KRYPTEIA

CHAPTER 1

THE TAKING

AGE 7

I WAS seven when they took me from my mother. She woke me in darkness, her hand shaking my shoulder the way she did when father came home drunk and we had to be quiet. But father had been two years in the ground, killed at Tanagra.

The hearth fire had burned down to embers. Cold seeped through the packed earth floor, through the goat-hair blanket, into bones still soft with growing. Our house had two rooms—one for living, one for the animals. The goats shifted in their pen, bleating low at the disturbance. Their smell mixed with smoke and the vinegar mother used to clean father's armor before she sold it.

She'd been grinding barley for three days, since the herald came. The sound had kept me awake—stone on stone, circular and endless. Every mother in the territory knew what that herald meant. The ephors needed boys. Some would die. Most would die. The survivors would become something useful.

She called me little wolf and told me to dress. Strange clothes—rough wool that scratched worse than our blankets, sandals cracked from previous wear. Another boy's sandals. He was ash now, or feeding worms.

When I reached for my wooden horse—the one father carved before Tanagra—she caught my wrist. The toy would stay here, she said. Her hand on my wrist stayed firm. She placed it on the shelf above our hearth.

You could see it in how she wouldn't meet my eyes. How she worked like a woman preparing a corpse. She'd started mourning me three days ago when the herald came. By the time Demetrios took me, she'd already burned me in her mind.

Outside, torches had gathered in the street. A woman pressed against a door frame, fingers clawing wood while her son was dragged past. The baker's wife argued with someone—voice rising until it cracked, then just wordless keening. The whole village bled children into the dark.

Demetrios stood big as a temple column. Scars ran up both arms like white snakes. Half his left ear was gone, chewed off raggedy. He'd been collecting boys for twenty years. You could see it in how he moved without urgency, how he looked through the women like they were already ghosts. We were just this season's harvest.

He told us our mothers had given us to Sparta. We'd become men or die. Most likely die. He said it the way a butcher tells sheep about the blade.

The baker's wife stepped forward. Said her boy was too young. Six summers. The law said seven.

Demetrios looked at the boy, told him to open his mouth. Counted teeth with a dirty finger. Adult teeth coming in. Good enough. Age was bones, not years. The compound measured everything in bone. Teeth for age. Ribs for starvation. Skulls for the tally.

The woman grabbed for her son. Demetrios backhanded her without looking. She hit the wall, slid down. Blood from her nose. She went quiet. Violence came without warning, without thought. Just function. I'd learn to deliver it the same way.

He told us tears marked us for death. The weak die first. Remember that or not.

We left as the eastern sky went gray. Six boys followed. At the second village, four more joined us. One had a black eye. Another kept looking back until Demetrios's stick taught him better. That boy lasted three days. Hope killed more of us than cold or hunger.

By the third village, nineteen of us marched together. At a crossroads shrine, eight more waited. Their village had bundled them early. Efficient.

Then a veteran approached, dragging his left leg. Bronze corselet patched with leather where spear points had found gaps. Missing two fingers on his shield hand. Said this was his son. They should take him.

Demetrios studied them. Asked where he'd served.

Mantinea, the veteran said. With the third lochos. Until a Theban blade found his leg.

Should have died there, Demetrios said.

The veteran's face went red. Started explaining—killed two before they brought him down, crawled back to the line. But Demetrios cut him off. Said the problem was the crawling back. Better men had stayed where they fell. Now this coward wanted the compound to fix his shame through his son.

But the compound didn't take volunteers from fathers trying to erase their own survival. It took boys whose mothers had already finished mourning them.

Demetrios's fist caught him in the mouth. The veteran went down hard, bad leg folding. Boot pressed on his chest, pressing him into dirt. Told him the dead at Mantinea were heroes. He was just a farmer with a limp and stories. His boy would stay here. Grow up knowing his father came back when better men fed the crows.

The boy stood frozen between them. That paralysis when you witness something irreversible and your body simply stops, unsure which way to move. I'd see that paralysis again—in boys watching mothers die, in men watching sons break.

We marched on. Ate barley cakes that turned to paste in your mouth. Water from a skin that tasted of leather and old wine. When boys asked for more, Demetrios laughed. The hungry learn faster than the fed, he said. Not that we'd learn to find food. We'd learn to function without it. Hunger would become our natural state. Anything above starvation was luxury.

An old woman followed us from the fourth village, screaming curses. Called Demetrios child-thief. Called the ephors worse. She threw a stone that caught him in the shoulder. He turned, studied her, kept walking. But I saw him touch the spot. Counting. Everything got counted—wounds, insults, debts. Twenty years later, I'd return to that village for the reckoning.

That night we slept in a field. No fire. Fire makes boys soft, Demetrios said. A boy from the market town wouldn't stop crying. Someone hit him. Then just breathing and wind in olive trees.

In the darkness, three boys tried to run. We heard them go—feet on grass, breathing that tried to be quiet. Then we heard Demetrios rise. Move after them. The sounds that followed were brief. Wet. When dawn came, he was cleaning his blade on grass while three shapes that had been boys cooled in the field. Runners die, he said. Remember or not.

The mountain rose ahead. By the time we reached the compound, we'd lost three more. One sat down and wouldn't get up. Demetrios checked him like examining livestock, then opened his throat. Another fell at the cliff turn. The third just disappeared. Gone was gone.

The compound walls appeared at sunset. Stone thick as a man is tall. Iron spikes on top caught dying light like teeth. The gates showed Artemis Orthia. Not the moon goddess mothers prayed to. The old thing that demanded blood. Fresh red painted around her mouth, still wet. The priests painted her before each collection. Fed her the idea of boys before feeding her the reality.

Thrasybulos stood by the gates counting us. Pale eyes. Bone amulets at his throat. Made marks on a wax tablet, touching the bones while counting. In ten years, he'd count six of us worthy of real work.

Seventy-two entered. I was number thirty-seven.

Inside, boys already there moved different. Shaved heads. Metal tags catching light at their throats. Gray tunics patched and re-patched. They looked at us the way wolves study rabbits. We were still soft. Still thought we might go home.

The compound would fix that. Would strip us of everything except function. Would teach us we weren't boys anymore. We were tools waiting to be sharpened. And tools don't feel. Don't remember. Don't hope.

They just cut.

CHAPTER 2

THE TAGS

THE MORNING after Demetrios delivered us to the compound, older boys stripped us in the courtyard. The burning pile smelled of wet wool and leather and something else—cedar oil from a rich boy's tunic, honey cakes someone had hidden in a pocket. Smoke thick enough to taste, bitter with whatever dyes the wealthy used. The older boys tore through our clothes—fingers inside seams, splitting sandal soles, unfolding cloak pins. They moved with practiced efficiency, boys who'd done this to others as it had been done to them.

One boy had sewn coins into his tunic hem. An older boy found them by weight, running the fabric between thumb and finger. A small carved horse tumbled from folded cloth. He flicked it into the fire without looking. All these small treasures fed the flames while we stood naked, sixty-something boys learning what it meant to own nothing.

The tags clinked against the smith's rod like wind chimes made of children's futures. Each piece was still warm from the forge when it touched our skin. Some boys jerked back from the heat. The smith just gripped harder, fingers finding that hollow below the throat where the tag would hang. He'd pressed ten thousand boys into the same position.

When my turn came, the heat was less than I'd expected but the weight was more. The filing system for bodies. But that day it was just weight where no weight had been before. The smith had arms like tree trunks, burn scars covering both forearms. Missing the middle finger on his right hand, the stump burned shut and shiny like melted wax.

Behind me, soft flesh met hot metal and someone whimpered. The smith made that wet clicking sound with his tongue—disapproval or just keeping count. The wine stench on his breath mixed with forge smoke and the smell of boys who'd pissed themselves during the mountain march and hadn't been allowed to wash.

Lysander watched the tagging with the same attention he'd give weapon inspection. Later he'd tell us our mothers had given us to Sparta, that names were privileges for citizens, not property. We'd answer to numbers or not at all. But that was lies. The instructors used our names when they beat us. We used each other's names fighting over bread. The numbers were for Thrasybulos's tablets, for the priests' records, for identifying bodies when the faces were gone.

But that first day we believed him.

After the tagging came the priests. Not the forge priest who'd blessed the tags—different ones for different purposes. The one who marked me had fingernails stained yellow from grinding laurel leaves, and when he leaned close, his breath was all bitter herbs and old wine. The ash mixture he pressed into my forehead burned cold. Made the skin pull tight like leather drying in sun. Behind him, another priest watched and made marks on a wax tablet—not writing, just symbols. Three overlapping circles for some boys. A spiral for others. Straight lines in different combinations. I got two vertical marks with a horizontal slash. Could have meant anything. Could have meant nothing. Maybe he was just making marks while the laurel smoke worked on his brain.

Helot boys distributed tunics. Rough wool that had been boiled but never softened. The fibers scraped raw skin where the mountain march had torn us up. Mine hung to my knees and smelled of lye and old vomit. You could see where previous boys had bled into the fabric—darker patches that washing couldn't remove.

An older boy led us to quarters. His tag was worn smooth from years against skin. He walked different than us—weight forward on his toes, hands never still, always touching walls and doorframes like he was counting. That constant counting would make sense later. Everything got counted here. Breaths. Steps. Deaths.

The sleeping hall could have held two hundred. We didn't half fill it. Straw mats in rows, compressed flat and sour with old sweat. In the corner where walls met floor, black mold grew in spreading fingers. The stones wept moisture that would freeze come winter, creating ridges of ice we'd learn to step over in darkness.

I found my assigned mat. Someone had scratched marks into the stone beside it—groups of seven vertical lines. Counting something worth the risk of punishment. Next to me, a boy sat on his mat shaking. Not fear shaking. Something else. His whole body locked and released in waves, muscles confused about whether to fight or collapse. Later I'd learn his name was Timomenes. Later still, I'd watch him freeze while Kyrillos failed to cut his mother's throat clean. But that night he was just the shape that whispered questions about food while his fingers grabbed straw in patterns—three grabs, pause, three grabs.

When the oil lamps guttered out, darkness came complete. Not the darkness of home where moon and stars leaked through shutters. This was architectural darkness, designed to swallow light. In it, boys made sounds they'd never make in daylight. Scratching—fingernails on stone. Someone muttering his village's protection chant again and again. Near the piss bucket, someone retching.

The tag had already worn a raw line around my neck. The weight pulled forward when I lay on my back, settled against my throat like a hand. I turned on my side. It shifted, found a new place to cut skin. Every position brought a different discomfort. The body learning to carry what it couldn't remove.

Somewhere in that darkness, a boy was listing the names of everyone in his village. Trying to hold onto them before they dissolved. Another was pulling threads from his tunic, counting them as they came loose. The soft boy who'd cried during tagging had gone silent—the dangerous kind of silent that meant something inside had shattered clean through.

The last thing I remember before sleep was the sound—dozens of tags shifting against chests as boys turned on their mats. Like coins in a purse. Like dice in a cup. Like small bells marking time until morning whistles taught us what those numbers really meant.

When morning came, the instructors dragged out two boys who'd cried in the night. We heard them in the courtyard—one begging, one singing a threshing song about separating grain. The singing stopped first. This was our first lesson about tears. We'd thought darkness meant privacy. We were wrong.

Metal shifted against bone, leather cords creaked as boys turned in darkness. The sound of boys learning they'd been counted, weighed, and found to be exactly what Sparta had paid for.

CHAPTER 3

THE ERRAND

AGE 8

THE COMPOUND SENT us into the world sometimes. Not to train. To be seen. To let citizens count their investment and helots remember their place.

Lysander gave me a leather cylinder and pointed west toward the temple of Demeter. Two hours' walk through settlements where citizens lived their soft lives. Past the perioikoi villages with their workshops and forges, free men who could own land but never vote, never train as we trained. Give this to the priest called Nikomedes. Wait for what he gives you. Come back.

An older boy dressed me in clean blue wool for the errand. Not compound gray that marked us as what we were, but the kind of tunic a farmer's son might wear to market. It fooled no one. The way I walked—weight on my toes, checking shadows—announced me louder than bronze bells. But the pretense mattered to someone.

At the first boundary stone, a merchant slowed his mule cart. Said he had room on the bench if I wanted to ride. His kindness lasted until I climbed up and he got a real look at me. Something in how I sat, how I watched the road ahead and behind at the same time. His throat worked like he was swallowing words.

He asked if I was from the place on the mountain.

I said nothing. But silence from boys like us was its own answer.

He said his cousin knew a man who'd worked construction up there. Said the man came back different. Wouldn't sleep indoors anymore. Counted everything— stones in the road, birds on roofs, teeth in his mouth. Seven times. Always seven. Said he'd seen boys eating their own dead during the bad winter. Said the priests fed us potions made from menstrual blood and ground bones to stop us feeling.

The merchant kept talking, filling the silence with every rumor he'd heard. The baby pit where the instructors threw the weak ones. The wolves that raised the survivors, teaching them to hunt in packs. How we could see in the dark because the priests had replaced our eyes with something else.

At the bridge, he told me to get down. His hand shook as he pressed a bronze obol into mine. For Hermes, he said. To blind my scent from honest folks.

I kept that obol for twenty-seven years. First coin someone gave me to go away. Carried it through all my

Provincial work until I lost it crossing to Athens when the Thirty took power. Probably still there at the bottom of the Saronic Gulf. Payment to leave decent people alone.

Three women stood at the crossroads shrine when I passed. Old women making their morning offerings. The eldest saw me first. She had the kind of face that had seen children die—loose skin and bitter lines and eyes that expected nothing good. She came forward, moving like her hips hurt but she wouldn't show it.

She said I had the look. Same dead eyes as her sister's boy before the compound took him. Three winters later the compound sent back a jar. Just ashes and milk teeth. But the teeth were wrong—too many for one boy. The priests had mixed the ashes, given families whatever filled the jar. She'd counted those teeth every night for years. Twenty-three small teeth that had come from multiple mouths.

Said the priests boiled boys who failed, used the broth to harden the ones who lived. Said that's why we moved different. Why we smelled like metal and sour milk. Why citizens' dogs went quiet when we passed.

She grabbed my wrist before I could stop her. Old woman's grip, all bones and tendons but stronger than expected. Turned my hand over to examine the scars on my palm from bronze practice. Her fingers traced the cuts like reading a map.

She said these were just the beginning. Said wait until the instructors started the real cutting. Channels carved in our backs for blood to run during temple ceremonies. Places for the goddess to drink from living fountains. Said her sister's boy had drawings of it before they took him—the patterns they'd carve, the way blood would flow from shoulder to hip.

The other two pulled her away. She kept talking as they dragged her back. Something about boys rutting in the wounds they made. Something about wombs full of bronze and salt. How Artemis Orthia drinks from mothers' eyes when their sons' teeth come back mixed with strangers'.

At the temple, two citizens argued near the treasury. The older one saw me first. Nudged his companion, nodded in my direction. They studied me like reading an inscription.

The younger one asked if I was one of the mountain boys.

He said his grandfather had helped design the compound. Proud of it, the way men are proud of well-built walls or clever drainage. Said the architects had cut special channels in the stone for all the blood. Gutters that fed the mountain itself. The goddess drank from below while priests drank from bowls. Very efficient.

The older one laughed. Said his grandfather told better stories. Said the physicians grafted wolf hearts into the strongest boys. Opened them up while they still breathed, replaced what made them human with what made them killers. That's why some survived wounds that would kill grown men. That's why we could smell fear-sweat at fifty paces. That's why our eyes reflected light in darkness.

He asked if I felt different inside. If the procedures had taken yet. Leaned in close like examining a half-butchered animal still breathing. His grandfather always wondered—did the surgeons cut out what was human or just bury it alive until it suffocated?

I said I was running an errand. Let my hand rest on my hip where a blade would hang in a few years.

He stepped back. Just one step, but we both heard it—the sound leather makes when a foot moves without meaning to. But he kept talking to the air beside me, voice going higher. Said maybe when I was older, when the physicians had finished the inside work, he could examine me properly. See if anything human was left rattling around in there or if it all got scooped out clean.

The priest Nikomedes took the cylinder without questions in the temple's inner chamber, where smoke from the morning's grain offerings still hung thick. Demeter's stone face watched from the wall—not the kind mother of Athens but the Spartan version with poppies and a sickle, marking harvest and sleep. Blood grooves ran from her altar to the drainage channel. Fresh stains said something had bled here at dawn.

He'd done this before. Boys from the compound appearing with sealed messages, leaving with whatever the priests traded in return. Part of some economy I didn't understand yet. While he prepared whatever Lysander wanted—I heard metal clicking against metal in the back room—his assistant wouldn't stop staring. Young man, maybe twenty, with the soft look of someone who'd never held bronze.

He asked quietly about his brother. Taken the year before I was born. No ashes returned. No confirmation. Just silence and the family pretending they'd only ever had one son. Asked if I knew what happened to the ones who didn't die clean. The suicides. The mad ones. The ones who broke wrong.

I told him we used different wood. Green pine that won't burn clean. Makes the smoke black and the ashes bitter. The disposal crews scatter them in the ravines where rain washes everything to nowhere.

He wanted specifics. Where. How. What happened to those ashes.

I said the ravines below the compound. Where everything broken ends up.

He nodded like that meant something. Like that was better than not knowing. Sometimes families just needed geography for their grief.

Walking back with whatever Nikomedes had sealed in the box—it rattled like metal on metal, or maybe teeth on teeth—I passed field workers breaking for water. Helots, moving in that careful way they had when citizens might be watching. But one old man broke from the group. Dangerous choice. The others watched him approach me with the kind of stillness that comes before violence.

He said we had a smell. Like metal and sour milk, just as the old woman had claimed. Said his father had taught him to recognize it. Said in his father's time, one of us had lived in their village for three months before the killing started. Shared their food. Learned their names. Learned their children's names. Then opened thirteen throats in one night, including the family that had sheltered him. Very clean work. Not wild killing. Targeted removal.

He asked if the compound taught us to pretend to be human or if some of us still remembered how.

He shuffled back to his group. They'd all stopped working to watch. Measuring distance. Checking if I was hunting or just passing through.

Near the last boundary stone, a citizen on horseback caught up. Good bronze, well-maintained. The kind carried by men who'd used it. Missing two fingers on his shield hand—clean cuts, not torn. War wounds, not work wounds.

He dismounted to get a better look at me. Studied my face like he was trying to see through skin to the scaffolding beneath. Asked if I was from the mountain. I nodded. No point pretending. He'd already recognized what I was.

He said good. Said six winters back, helots had broken into his farm. Held him down. Made him watch while they used his wife and daughter. Would have killed them all but someone saw smoke from the burning barn and raised the alarm.

Said two boys like me had tracked them for six days. Found them in a shepherd's hut near Sellasia. What those boys did took all night. He'd heard the screams from his position with the recovery party. Said when the unit finally went in at dawn, the helots had forgotten every god's name but one.

His wife never spoke again. Something broken in her throat or maybe just her mind. But she lived. His daughter too. She'd had children since. They played in the same yard where it happened. That was because of us. Because boys like me knew how to make men die so badly that other helots still wake up screaming about it.

He reached into his purse. I stepped back. We couldn't take payment. He knew that. Said he wasn't offering coin. Just wanted me to know that some citizens understood. The helots outnumbered them forty to one. Without us, every Spartan family would suffer like his had. Every wife. Every daughter. Every son who couldn't defend what mattered.

He asked if I'd started field work yet.

I said no.

He said when I did, to remember that every throat we opened meant a citizen child slept safer. We subtracted so they could add.

Fifteen years later I saw him in Megara. His daughter walking the market with twin boys grown tall. She had his way of checking shadows. The mother nowhere to be seen. Still couldn't speak, probably. Or dead from the kind of silence that eats you from inside.

The box from Nikomedes rattled with each step. When I gave it to Lysander, he opened it immediately. Bronze needles for the scarification ceremonies, wrapped in lamb's wool. Two dozen, different lengths. The priest had included extra, like always. Some of the senior boys would palm them during inventory. Trade them for food, for advantages, for silence about things done in darkness. Lysander knew. The priest knew. Everyone pretending not to know because that too was part of the economy.

Lysander held one needle up to the light, testing its point against his thumb until blood beaded. He asked which story the old women were telling this season—the one about drinking boys' blood or the one about fucking the wounds we carved.

I told him the merchant gave me coin to go away. The old woman counted her sister's teeth. The helot knew about the thirteen throats. And they all said we smell like metal and sour milk.

He held one needle up to the light, checking its point. Said let them tell their stories. Made them watch their children closer. Made them count their kitchen knives. Made them bar their doors tighter. Fear was useful. The wrong kind of fear was wasteful, but the right kind—the fear that we might be watching—that kept people careful.

He asked which story I believed.

I said the one about the drains.

He made a sound that might have been a laugh if men like him laughed. Said the drains were real. Cut special to handle the flow. Everything else was what people needed to believe to explain what we were. Made us into demons or god-touched or cursed when really we were just boys who'd been pressed through stone until only the useful parts came out the other side.

CHAPTER 4

THE MEAT CIRCLE

AGE 8

THE COMPOUND TAUGHT us to fight like dogs before teaching us to fight like men.

Lysander had us form a circle in the sand pit. The sand burned bare feet if you stood still, but standing still wasn't going to be an option. No weapons. No armor. Just boys learning what violence felt like skin to skin.

This was pankration day. All-power. Everything allowed except eyes and killing blows. Winner stays, fresh meat enters. Fight until someone yields or the instructors pull you apart.

We understood. This wasn't about technique. This was about finding out who froze when fists started flying and who went empty enough to function.

Nikos first. Still thick despite the starvation rations. Then Stephanos. Coastal boy, quick the way hunger makes you quick.

Neither knew how to start. Every morning we drilled with weapons. Now just empty hands and permission to hurt each other.

Stephanos raised his fists like tavern fighters. Nikos just lowered his head and charged.

Just mass hitting mass. They went down, Nikos on top through sheer weight. Wild punches that mostly found sand. But one caught Stephanos's ear—wet meat hitting stone. His eyes lost focus for that heartbeat when your brain bounces off your skull.

Stephanos grabbed Nikos's hair, tore some loose. They rolled in sand, learning that fighting hurt both ways.

This was the real lesson. Not how to fight—they'd teach that later. But what happened when technique disappeared. When it was just your meat against someone else's.

Nikos's fist caught Stephanos's nose. Blood exploded across both faces. First understanding this was real.

Lysander called stop.

Nikos kept swinging. Lost in it already.

Lysander's stick cracked across his spine. Hard enough to break the pattern. They pulled Stephanos up—nose bent sideways, blood mixing with sand. The grinding sound of cartilage finding new positions.

Fresh meat. Dimitri from the mountain villages.

They crashed together. Dimitri went low, got Nikos around the knees. Good position but no idea what to do with it. Just held on while Nikos hammered his back.

Then Dimitri bit him. Hard. Thigh above the knee. Locked on like a dog with a bone.

Lysander called stop.

Dion told us no biting. Said fight like men, not animals. But we weren't men. We were boys taught that everything was allowed except eyes and death.

Fresh meat. Kyrillos.

No planning. Just throwing fists. One caught Nikos's stomach by luck. Nikos drove him down, started hammering with the bottom of his fist. Kyrillos got a knee up between Nikos's legs—not aimed, just flailing. But it found its mark. Nikos gasped, rolled away. Kyrillos scrambled on top, grabbed his throat.

Not a proper choke. Just strangling. Nikos's face went purple.

Lysander hauled Kyrillos off. When I say stop, you stop.

Kyrillos tried to get up, still lost in the fight. Lysander knocked him out cold. Precise temple strike.

Lysander looked at Nikos, gasping on the ground. Said Nikos stays in.

But Nikos could barely stand. Fresh meat kept coming.

I watched patterns emerge. Boys who went for throats first. Boys who froze when blood touched their faces. Each fight teaching what worked.

When Lysander pointed at me, half our group had taken beatings. He paired me with a hill boy who'd survived three rounds. Exhausted. Blood from his nose painting him like a priest of Ares. I didn't know how to fight, but I knew tired when I saw it.

I rushed him. We collided, both swinging. His fist caught my eye—white light exploding. We grabbed each other, wrestling stupid. I hooked his ankle by accident. We went down.

I landed on top, started hitting. No leverage—weak slaps. He bucked, threw me off. Got on top.

I panicked. Pushed at his face with my thumbs. He bit one. Deep. I screamed, yanked free. First time I'd been bitten by another human. Worse than being hit. More personal.

He tried for my throat. I tucked my chin, got my legs around him. Squeezed.

Lysander called stop.

I'd won by being less tired. Nothing more.

Fresh meat entered. The violence evolved. Still wild, but purposeful now. Boys targeting what they'd seen work.

My second round, something had changed. My opponent went straight for my throat. I tucked my chin. He grabbed my ear, tried to tear it off. I bit his wrist. We circled, both adapting.

He came low. We went down hard. I got on top, started hitting. Just fists finding meat. Each impact shocked up my arms but I kept swinging.

Lysander called stop.

I heard it distant, like sound through water. My fists kept working.

Lysander called stop again. Louder.

Still couldn't stop. The violence had me.

Then pain exploded through my body. Started at my neck, shot down my spine.

My whole body locked up. Frozen with every nerve on fire.

Lysander had me. Two fingers pressed into my neck. He lifted me off the ground with just that grip.

When I say stop, you stop.

He held me there. Showing everyone.

You fight with rage. Rage makes you stupid. Stupid gets you dead.

His knee came up into my stomach. Controlled but brutal. Again. My insides turned to paste. Again.

He dropped me. I curled around my destroyed stomach, vomiting bile.

When I finally pushed up, Kyrillos helped me back to the circle. No words. The compound was teaching us helping was weakness. But some habits died slower.

By midday, every boy had fought twice. We looked like we'd been thrown off cliffs. Split lips, torn hair, bite marks. One boy's ear hung half-off where I'd tried to tear it.

We sat in the dust while Lysander explained what we'd learned. But we already knew. Control beat rage. And when someone said stop, you stopped.

Or you learned why.

CHAPTER 5

THE FIRST LESSON

AGE 8

DAWN RAIN still made the eastern courtyard stones black when they lined up six helots for our first killing lesson. They gave us real bronze for the first time. My hands shook when I took the blade. The body's knowledge that it was about to cross a line that couldn't be uncrossed.

They'd divided us into groups. Four boys per helot, each would cut once, pass the blade, learn through doing what months of practice on wooden posts had only mimicked. My group got a man maybe thirty, harvest worker from the calluses ground so deep into his hands that dirt had become part of the skin. When the drunk priest marked his forehead with ash and oil, the man spoke just one word. Nikias.

Maybe his son. Maybe his brother. Maybe just the last sound a dying mouth could make. A name I'd pass on to a tax collector in Gythium, recycling death like bronze through a forge.

Lysander demonstrated on another helot first. Grip, angle, pressure—bronze sliding smooth under ribs, angled up to find the heart. Three heartbeats from cut to dead. Professional work that made killing look like any other craft that could be mastered through repetition.

Alexios went first in our group. Baby fat still on his cheeks, his mother's honey cakes just a memory now. His cut was shallow, tentative—barely through skin across the shoulder. The helot didn't even flinch, just kept watching those mountains like they might walk over and carry him away. Dion's stick cracked across Alexios's knuckles. Deeper. With purpose.

The second cut found muscle. Blood welled dark and steady. The helot's breathing changed—shorter, careful, the way men breathe around broken ribs. Still not dying. Still watching mountains.

Then my turn. The blade handle was slick with sweat and blood, heavier than in practice. I remember thinking I should go for the kidney—Dion had shown us on practice dummies, that soft spot in the lower back. Quick death if you hit it right.

I went in wrong. Too high, hit something hard—bone or cartilage. The helot jerked, made a sound like old leather tearing. His legs did something I'd never seen before— still moved but different, like puppet strings had tangled. I'd hit spine, found some bundle of nerves that disconnected his lower body from his will. He tried to turn, to see what I'd done, but his waist down had gone foreign to him.

Dion grabbed my wrist, adjusted the angle. Said kidneys hide deeper than you think. Push through the fear of going too deep.

But I'd already changed something fundamental in that man. When I pulled the blade out, clear fluid came with the blood—the water that bathes the spine, the stuff that keeps bone from grinding bone. His legs kept twitching, separate from his control. Meat and will failing to connect.

In Ephesus, fifteen years on, I'd use the same cut on a merchant who'd been selling garrison schedules. Let him stumble around the agora for three days, legs not quite working, while his partners realized he'd been marked. But at eight, it was an accident that turned a man into a demonstration of how completely we could unmake someone without quite killing them.

Nikos took the blade next, opened the helot's side with farm-boy strength. Intestines pushed against the wound from inside, gray-pink through the gap. The smell hit— shit and iron and something sour that meant we'd reached the inner workings. By then our man was trying to crawl despite his ruined legs, upper body pulling while the lower dragged behind like wet rope.

When Castor's turn came, he froze. Stood there with the blade shaking in his grip while behind us another group was finishing—their helot had died quick from someone finding the great vessel. Blood painted the stones in pulsing jets. One boy from that group was on his knees vomiting. The sound made two others start.

Castor finally struck—wild swing that caught the helot's neck but wrong. Not the vessels, just muscle. The man screamed then. First real scream of the morning. High and raw. The instructors cataloged which boys hesitated, which struck too hard, which looked away.

Lysander stepped down from his platform, took the blade from Castor. One thrust under the jaw, up into the brain. No wasted movement. Perfect technique that showed why he taught and we learned. The helot dropped, legs finally stopped their twitching, and Nikias —whoever that was—went unspoken into smoke.

But Lysander studied me. Said I'd found something useful by accident. Something worth remembering.

Two boys couldn't do it—their bodies locked when they tried to raise the blade. They'd go to the kitchens. Three boys kept staring at the bodies after, wanted to cut again.

We dragged the corpses to the burning ground. The paralyzed helot was heaviest—dead weight is different when you caused it.

By spring, first blood was just memory. The shaking stopped after the third killing. The hesitation after the fifth. By the tenth, we could eat immediately after, bronze still wet on our hands. We'd killed dozens more, gotten better, cleaner. The compound had ground us into new shapes through repetition.

But I still remember that first helot watching mountains while we made him die in pieces. How his legs had twitched separate from his will. How Nikias—son or brother or just a final sound—had been his last word. Some boys discovered they couldn't do it. Some discovered they liked it. Most of us found the middle emptiness where it was just work.

CHAPTER 6

THE FIRST WINTER

THE COMPOUND GAVE us just enough food that first winter to see who'd eat their own dead.

Morning barley mush. Evening bread hard enough to break teeth. Calculated portions—not enough to thrive, too much to die clean. The compound wanted us desperate, not dead. Yet.

Three boys froze before the real hunger started. We found them at morning count, ice crystals in their open eyes. They weighed nothing. Weeks of measured starvation had already consumed everything except what was needed to keep breathing. Their bodies had burned through fat first, then muscle, then whatever makes a person want to keep going. By the end they were just architecture wrapped in skin.

The mad ones came first. Boy who kept asking about eyeless goats. Another who counted to seven over and over, rocking in place. When the counter tried to sleep near me for warmth, I could hear him whisper: Seven knives, seven throats, seven boys in seven pieces. His breath stank of ketosis—that sweet-rot smell when a body starts eating itself.

Then came Barley-Mush Morning—what we called the day someone found fingers in their bowl. Not whole fingers. Chunks. Knuckle joints floating in the gray paste like dumplings made wrong. Someone had taken them from the boy who'd frozen, hidden them, added them to the pot when the servers weren't watching. Extra protein from a source that wouldn't fight back.

The finger-eater gave himself away by not reacting. Everyone else gagged, pushed their bowls away. He kept eating. Methodical. Chewing around the bones with the patience of someone who'd already made peace with what survival required. When he noticed us staring, he shrugged. Said meat's meat. Said it like explaining water was wet.

That's when the counting boy snapped. Launched himself at the finger-eater, screaming about seven bodies for seven dinners. They rolled through frozen piss, both past sanity. The counter got his teeth into the finger-eater's throat. Tore out everything important in one pull. Kept chewing while the finger-eater bled out. The sound —wet and gristled, like a dog working through cartilage.

Swallowed.

Lysander broke the counter's neck himself. Quick twist. Professional. The kind of economy that said he'd done this before, would do it again. But I saw him checking the corpse's fingers after. Counting. Making sure all ten were there. Even instructors had limits.

They locked us down after that. No movement between quarters and common areas without escort. Guards at every door—older boys who'd survived their own winters, who knew exactly what hunger could make us do. They searched our mats while we stood in formation, breath steaming in the cold while they tore through our few possessions.

Most boys had nothing. Some had hoarded bread crusts, dried berries, things that might keep them one day further from eating the dead. They confiscated it all, making careful notes about who'd hidden what. Another data point in whatever experiment they were running.

But they passed over certain mats without searching. Boys who'd proven useful in other ways. Boys whose information networks or special skills bought them exemptions. I memorized which mats they skipped, understanding another economy at work. Starvation was just one currency. Information was another.

Two days later, parts of both boys were missing. Clean cuts at the joints. Someone had learned from the finger-eater's mistake—take from the fresh dead, cook it properly, mix it with your own rations where no one could see. Professional butchery from boys who'd only learned anatomy through violence.

That night, I couldn't sleep. The compound had gone too quiet—that particular silence when everyone's awake, listening, waiting for the next horror to reveal itself. My mat felt colder than the stone beneath it. Around me, boys breathed in careful rhythms, each pretending sleep while staying ready to defend their nothing from others with nothing.

A rat scratched behind the wall near Nikos's mat. Strange, because rats had been scarce since the real hunger started. We'd eaten most of them. Caught them with string snares, twisted their necks, roasted them over oil lamp flames when the guards weren't watching. Even the taste of rat was better than the taste of empty.

I crept over to investigate. My knees knew every cold stone between my mat and his, which ones would creak under weight, which held puddles of ice-melt. The sound was coming from behind a loose stone where Nikos slept. Not a rat—too regular, too deliberate. My fingers found the gap, worked the stone free with the patience of someone who understood that discovery meant death.

Inside: bread, dried meat, and something that made my empty stomach clench—a child's finger bone, still wrapped in tendon. Small as a spring pea. Too small to have come from any of us. The kitchen boys. He'd been trading with kitchen boys, and one had paid him in the only meat they could steal. From the infant pyres where Sparta burned the weak before they could grow.

I stared at that small bone, understanding flooding through me like ice water. Nikos had his own economy, his own network. While we starved in the open, he'd been trading information or services for food. And someone in the kitchens had gotten desperate enough to pay with the only meat they had access to. The meat that came pre-cooked from the burning grounds.

The cache was organized. Careful. Bread wrapped in cloth to keep it from molding. Meat dried and portioned. Everything except that finger bone, which sat apart like an accusation. Or a promise of what lines could be crossed when the mush ran thin.

I put everything back exactly as I'd found it. Each item in its place. Sealed the stone with the same slow care I'd used to open it. Crept back to my mat carrying knowledge that felt heavier than any meal. But now I knew— there were layers to the compound's economy I hadn't seen. Boys trading in currencies I hadn't imagined.

Within days, the compound had measured exactly how much hunger it took to make boys eat boys. Theron never moved from his wall during the worst of it. Just sat there with those calculating eyes, watching who broke and how. But afterwards, he knew exactly who'd eaten human meat. Who'd hesitated. Who'd fought hardest for the scattered food. He traded that information to the instructors for tiny advantages—an extra ladle here, a warmer spot there. Survival through observation rather than violence.

The weak ones died faster after that. Pushed to the edges where the cold bit deepest. No shared warmth. No warnings about bad ice. They faded while the valuable ones—

the ones who'd eaten flesh without hesitation or found other ways to feed—survived.

By the time snow melted, twenty percent of us were gone. Frozen, starved, murdered, or driven mad enough that murder was mercy. The compound had watched it all. Counted who broke which way. Sorted us by what we'd swallow. Filed us into categories: will eat the dead, won't eat the dead, will trade for the dead, will kill for the chance to eat.

Later, Theron would catalog Athens the same way. Watch who'd betray whom for advantage. He'd die rich because he'd learned that winter that everyone breaks— you just need to watch close enough to see the fault lines. But he'd learned it here first, watching boys decide between starvation and damnation.

But I survived because I ate my rats whole and didn't ask what meat Nikos was trading. Because when I found that infant bone, I put it back and took the bread. Because the compound was teaching us everything was edible if you were empty enough. And because I learned that some knowledge was more dangerous than hunger.

The thaw revealed bones we'd missed in the snow. The priests counted them, making notes about which parts were missing. Adding up what we'd subtracted from each other to survive. Their tablets would show the arithmetic: seventy-two boys minus twenty percent equals tools worth keeping. The rest was just winter's work, cleaning out the weak before spring brought new horrors.

CHAPTER 7

THE KEEPER'S TALE

AGE 8

WE CRAWLED on hands and knees across the barracks floor, sorting teeth. Four hundred and thirty-six fragments scattered across stone—some still pink with tissue, others brown with age. My fingers found one tiny as a grain of barley. Could only have come from an infant. I held it longer than I should have.

Thrasybulos told us to sort them. Adult molars in one pile. Children's teeth in another. His walking stick tapped stone with each word, carved from wood taken from the scaffold where Sparta had hanged Nikias twenty years back. The compound made all their ceremonial objects from the instruments of their enemies' deaths.

The teeth clicked against each other like dice as we sorted. A molar with a gold filling—someone who'd had wealth once. A row of perfect white incisors from someone young. Three tiny teeth that must have come from the same child's mouth.

Marcus asked why we were doing this.

Thrasybulos picked up a child's tooth, turned it in the lamplight like examining a gem. This one had asked his mother why helots work while citizens train. She told him stories about when Messenia belonged to itself. The boy repeated these stories to other children. Within a month, playground games had turned into tiny rebellions.

He dropped the tooth into our pile. It landed with a sound like a thrown die.

The teeth came from a village above Sellasia. Summer clearing, he called it. Sixty-seven helots who'd been meeting at night, speaking old Messenian. The language of free men, not slaves.

I found another infant's tooth. Smaller than the first. Added to the pile.

Nikias had united three villages twenty years back. Started with reasonable requests—less grain taken, fewer work days. But reasonable requests became demands. Demands became resistance. Resistance became revolution. Sparta hanged four hundred in one morning. Made the families watch.

Thrasybulos's walking stick had been carved from the scaffold that held Nikias's weight. Now it tapped against stone as he explained how that name lived on. Parents named their sons Nikias like a prayer for rebellion. Like naming them Remember. Like naming them Rise Again.

Every helot child called Nikias was a small act of defiance, a whispered hope that another leader might emerge.

That's why we kept hearing it from dying lips. That's why it appeared scratched on wax tablets, gasped by tax collectors, whispered by women watching their children taken. The name had become more than memory—it had become promise. And promises, Thrasybulos said, were just another thing that needed cutting out.

Thrasybulos scratched numbers in the dirt with his stick. Eight thousand citizens. Three hundred sixty thousand helots. For every Spartan who could hold a spear, forty-five helots held in bondage. Let that ratio reach sixty to one, the system collapses. Drop it to twenty to one through excess killing, not enough labor to feed anyone.

We kept sorting while he talked. My pile of children's teeth grew. Some with roots still attached—torn out, not fallen naturally. One still had dried blood in the crevices.

He said we were learning to find the exact measure of blood that kept the world arranged as the gods intended. Five hundred removed annually in good years. Eight hundred when unrest spread. Always the right five hundred—the ones who asked questions, who remembered old songs, who might unite others.

A helot brought a bucket, set it down careful, backed away fast. The smell hit—brine and iron and meat going soft. Thrasybulos dumped the contents onto our sorted piles.

Eyes. Maybe two dozen, floating in salt water, trailing pink threads where Provincial boys had torn them from sockets.

He said these came from the mothers who'd organized burials after the teeth-pulling. Who'd formed a burial society to share grief. That grief had turned to anger. Anger to plans. These women had been teaching their children the old songs, the old counting methods. Teaching them they were something other than property.

So Provincial units took their eyes. Not killed—blinded. Women who now needed constant care, draining resources, reminding everyone daily of the cost of remembering. Death made martyrs. Maiming made expenses.

We had to sort these too. Right eyes. Left eyes. Some obvious—the tear duct placement. Others impossible to tell, just gray-white spheres floating in brine.

When we finished, the piles told their own lesson. Adult teeth outnumbered children's three to one—Sparta preferred to remove problems before they could breed more problems. The eyes were all from women of child-bearing age. Precision in everything.

The drunk priest arrived as we completed the sorting. Not the usual one whose hands shook unless they held bronze. A younger one who knew the blood rites.

He paired us as blood brothers. Opened my palm with his blade deep enough to show yellow fat beneath.

Kyrillos cut his to match. The priest caught our blood in a clay bowl while we stood among sorted teeth and floating eyes. Added sour wine and salt, made us drink while our blood swirled together like smoke in water.

Thrasybulos explained while the priest worked. What one failed, both would answer for. What one began, the other must finish. The compound didn't create brotherhood—it created accountability systems. When one tool broke, the other would be marked by association.

Seven years later, I'd keep that promise with my eating knife, cutting Kyrillos down from the beam he'd measured a thousand times. But that night we were just boys learning that even our blood belonged to the compound's economy.

Everything had secondary purpose. The teeth would be ground for bonemeal. The eyes would go to the Egyptian for his experiments. Our blood-bond would ensure that when Kyrillos started measuring roof beams, I'd be obligated to watch. To document. To fulfill whatever promise the compound decided our mixed blood meant.

And the name Nikias would echo through our work, through dying gasps, through children's practice letters, until one day I'd wear it myself in Athens—the ultimate corruption. A Spartan weapon bearing the name of Sparta's greatest helot rebel. Thrasybulos would probably appreciate the irony, if men like him understood irony as anything more than another tool.

That scar on my palm never faded right. Even now, I can trace where the priest bound me to Kyrillos. Made us responsible for each other's function until hemp and prophecy separated us.

By dawn, we understood. We were the balance. We were the arithmetic. And someday, we'd be counted too.

CHAPTER 8

THE EDUCATION

AGE 11

LYSANDER BROUGHT three broken specialists to the compound on the same morning. The Egyptian with his missing fingers, Damon who counted on a hand missing its middle digit, and Dionysios who taught anatomy between swigs of wine. We'd rotate between them hourly. No rest. No processing. Just function while drowning in different kinds of death.

Forty-eight of us split into three groups. My group went to Dionysios first.

The anatomy hall wept constant water from its walls. A helot lay strapped to the demonstration platform, still breathing. Dionysios ate figs while explaining where to cut. Sweet fruit mixed with copper blood—that combination would stay with me forever.

He opened the man sternum to pelvis. The helot's eyes stayed fixed on the ceiling while his belly split like over-ripe fruit. Dionysios called five boys down. Made us put our hands inside while the man still breathed. The heart beat against my palm, confused by air it was never meant to feel. Kyrillos's hand found the same organ from the other side. For a moment, we both held that failing heart between us. Same recognition. Same understanding of what we were becoming. Then the heart stuttered, stopped.

Dionysios kept working, showing kidney placement. Said we'd eat what we studied at evening meal. Wiped his hands on his bloody apron and took another fig.

The poison room reeked of bitter almonds. The Egyptian waited with his tables of plants, bronze scales, mortars arranged precisely. Three fingers missing on his left hand—paid to temples for knowledge. Careful amputation, not violence. The price of learning which plants killed fastest.

He spoke damaged Greek. Said the blade was honest. Poison was a liar that killed while you drank wine elsewhere. He crushed wolfsbane while explaining. Root strongest, then leaf, then flower.

We still tasted organ meat when he made us weigh death on scales fine enough to count eyelashes. One grain too much, too fast. One grain too little, just sickness. Dimitri's hands shook measuring his dose. Three grains over. The Egyptian made him drink it diluted—just enough to teach.

Within fifty heartbeats, Dimitri was on his knees. Vomit and shit pouring out while his pupils went black. The

Egyptian counted symptoms on his remaining fingers, completely detached. At two hundred heartbeats exactly, he gave charcoal water. Made Dimitri drink until the vomiting turned black.

Behind us, screams from the anatomy hall. Next group's demonstration had started.

Third rotation. Damon looked like someone who counted grain—short, weak chin, oiled hair. But when he moved, even the compound dogs went silent. His missing middle finger created a gap when he counted. The gap bothered him. You could see him pause, expecting touch that never came.

His voice came out barely above whisper. He grabbed Dimitri—still weak from poison—to demonstrate. Said weakness made better practice. Showed us the blood choke. Dimitri's eyes rolled back in ten seconds. Damon held him under for thirty, explaining the progression. Consciousness, damage, death. Released him. Dimitri dropped, pissed himself, woke up confused.

Then we practiced on each other. Marcus went too hard, crushed something in Philippos's throat. Not quite the windpipe but close. Philippos spent the rest of the day breathing like he was drowning in air.

My partner was Castor. When he got the choke position, I tasted wolfsbane comeback mixed with blood from his unwashed hands. The world went gray at the edges. Then warm darkness. Then I was on the ground with piss running down my legs.

By noon, the divisions blurred. In the poison room, the Egyptian explained hemlock while we could hear wet impacts from anatomy—Dionysios demonstrating how to crack a sternum. My hands shook measuring nightshade while remembering the temperature of a living heart.

Kitchen boys fed us during the sixth hour. The meat had specific grain. We knew exactly which demonstration subject we were eating because we'd felt those same muscles resist when pulling organs free. I identified kidney by texture. The iron-rich liver. Even heart, chopped fine but recognizable by density.

Dimitri couldn't keep it down. Still poisoned, now trying to digest what he'd just had his hands inside. The Egyptian watched him vomit with professional interest.

But Dimitri never recovered from that lesson. Within a week, he'd developed the full ritual—smell first, then lip test, then tongue, then counting fifty breaths before swallowing. The compound noticed, started moving his rations to different boys, testing whether hunger would override caution. It didn't. He'd go two days without eating rather than accept bread from someone he hadn't watched prepare it.

By our third year, he'd become something between joke and warning. The boy who'd learned the wrong lesson. His paranoia was about ingestion. Only ingestion. He'd fight without hesitation, take beatings without flinching. It was the invisible threats—the maybe-poison in every meal—that consumed him.

In the pit, he'd die with his eyes on the other prisoners' hands, watching for hidden powders, while thumbs found what paranoia had blinded him to.

That afternoon, the specialists combined lessons. Damon had us practice chokes on boys the Egyptian had given mild doses to. See how poison changed the timing. Meanwhile, Dionysios worked on a fresh corpse, showing how strangulation deaths displayed specific organ damage.

Kyrillos broke during the eighth hour. Just stopped moving during poison grinding. Stood there with pestle in hand, staring at nothing. The Egyptian slapped him. Nothing. The instructors sent him to kitchen duty. Within the hour, three more boys followed.

I kept functioning by cataloging everything. Technical details that let me avoid thinking about what we were becoming. Around me, boys found their own ways to continue. Theron took notes. Nikos went aggressive, volunteering for every demonstration. Marcus counted everything in sevens.

By evening, we'd lost eight boys to madness or breaking. The rest of us sat in the common hall, exhausted beyond description. Kitchen staff served us organ soup. We ate without speaking, too tired to recognize what we consumed.

That night in quarters, boys made sounds they'd never make in daylight. Alexios kept listing plant names. Someone practiced the wet breathing of a crushed windpipe. In the corner, a boy strangled himself with his own hands—not suicide, just practice.

I lay counting. Four hundred thirty breaths between watch bells. If I focused on the counting, I couldn't taste the copper. Couldn't feel the heart beating against my palm.

The compound wanted to see who could drown in all of it at once and keep breathing. Who could hold poison knowledge while their hands were wrist-deep in human cavity. Who could practice strangulation with wolfsbane still burning his throat.

The three specialists left together at week's end. But we kept what they'd taught. The Egyptian's patience with measurement. Damon's finger-counting of consciousness fading. Dionysios's casual dismantling of human architecture.

That was the real lesson. Not the individual skills but the ability to perform while drowning in horror. To keep working when our minds wanted to shatter like the boys sent to kitchens.

The compound had shown us what we were—not boys learning to be killers, but empty vessels being filled with different kinds of death. The ones who could hold it all without spilling would continue. The rest would wash pots until rope or madness took them.

CHAPTER 9

THE ORACLE

Thrasybulos summoned three of us to his chambers on a morning when frost still clung to the eastern stones. Me, Kyrillos, and Marcus, chosen for reasons we wouldn't understand until later.

The mantis lived three days into the mountains, he told us. Used to serve at Delphi until he misread an omen and the god took his left eye. Now he read futures in living meat.

The chamber was sparse except for an amphora on the desk. Black-figure work showing men being devoured, their faces peaceful as lions tore them open. When Kyrillos shifted weight off his left foot (still favored it from the mountain march two years back), our instructor's eyes tracked the movement. Just a scratch in wax, another observation recorded.

From beneath the amphora, he pulled a hide map stained with what might have been old blood or just weather. No place names, just charcoal marks showing ridges, water sources, caves. His finger traced a path that ended at a circle with three dots inside.

The mantis kept two servants. A woman who remembered everything she heard, her tongue split into three parts to hold more words. And a giant born with joints that bent in directions that made you sick to watch. We'd need to speak certain words at the cave mouth or the giant would break us just to see what sounds we made.

The words came out wrong when we tried them. Not Greek. Not any language meant for human throats. Just wet consonants that hurt to speak. Again and again until our mouths could form them properly, while morning sun crept across the floor and the amphora's painted lions watched us practice sounds that would keep us alive.

The map led us through game trails and water channels cut by spring melt. The amphora took turns breaking our shoulders. Good wine weighs more than piss wine. Marcus carried it the first day, rope cutting those same channels where his childhood pack had worn grooves. By the second day, his shoulders were bleeding through his tunic.

Third morning, we found the ridge overlooking the valley. Shaped like a cupped hand waiting to be filled. Smoke rose from the cave mouth, but wrong smoke. Too thick, too yellow, carrying herbs that made your lungs close if you breathed deep. Below, three wooden frames stood X-shaped against the morning light. Things hung on them. Ravens picked at the shapes.

We watched for an hour before descending. Marcus kept checking exits, cataloging escape routes even here where escape meant nothing. The movement below had patterns: three figures working between cave and frames. One huge, ducking to enter the cave mouth. One draped in robes that dragged channels in the dirt. One naked except for a rope belt, tools hanging from it that caught sunlight.

The wind shifted and brought the smell. Rot and burned herbs and something else. The stench of men kept alive past the point where death would be mercy. Marcus's jaw worked like he was trying not to gag.

At fifty paces, the frames showed clear. Men. Or had been. The freshest still moved, slow twisting like wind-caught laundry. The other two had stopped moving but hadn't stopped serving their purpose. Ravens had taken the soft parts. Empty sockets tracked our approach better than living eyes would have.

The moving one had no eyelids. Sun had baked his eyes to leather, but they still tracked our movement. Still aware. The middle frame held a man opened from sternum to pelvis, ribs spread like wings, organs arranged outside his body in patterns that meant something to someone. The third was mostly bones held together by dried sinew, but the bones had been carved with symbols. Even dead, he was still being written on.

The naked man emerged when we got within ten paces. Left eye socket empty, just a hole that wept yellow down his cheek. Scars covered his body in deliberate patterns.

Not battle wounds but ritual markings. The rope belt held bronze tools. Small blades. Probes. Things for getting inside without killing too quick.

I spoke the words Thrasybulos had taught us. They came out wrong, tongue catching on sounds that wanted to cut my throat from inside. The giant appeared in the cave mouth, head tilted at an angle that made my neck hurt just watching. Joints bent backward at knee and elbow.

I tried the words again. Got them right. The giant's head straightened with a sound like knuckles cracking in sequence. Moved aside.

The woman came out next. When she spoke, I understood about the split tongue. Not split. Separated. Three distinct parts that moved independently, letting her speak in layers. She said the moon was right, the mountain had sent us, to bring the wine.

Inside the cave, smoke made everything uncertain. A brass bowl held coals that glowed without flame. The walls were covered in tablets. Thousands of clay rectangles marked with symbols. Some showed wounds in anatomical detail. Others showed patterns I couldn't read then but recognize now: the counting marks of boys who'd visited, who'd lived, who'd hanged themselves or opened their veins or found other ways to make prophecy true.

The mantis sat on woven grass, empty socket weeping steadily while his good eye studied us. Behind him, passages led deeper into the mountain. Metal scraped stone back there. Breathing sounds that weren't quite human.

We set down the wine. He took the amphora immediately, drank deep. Good wine to wash down the smoke. Payment for prophecies, though we'd been the ones paying with our backs. He drank like a man who'd been waiting, throat working as he swallowed. When he lowered it, wine mixed with the yellow pus from his weeping socket, creating ribbons of pink down his cheek.

He asked what Thrasybulos wanted to know.

I gave the prepared words. Syracuse. Bronze and glory. Would the gods favor Spartan arms?

The mantis made a sound that might have been laughter if laughter came from a throat full of glass. Said Thrasybulos had sent boys who smelled like burial. Said he'd answer the questions we brought but we'd hear the questions we didn't ask.

He stood. Took a blade from his belt. Not harvest-ready bronze but something older, green with patina except where the edge had been kept sharp. Went to the cave mouth where morning light made everything too bright.

He worked on the one with no eyelids. Made three cuts. Shallow, the kind that would bleed slow. The hanging man jerked but couldn't close his eyes. Couldn't stop watching the blade open his flesh. The mantis pressed harder, found something that made the man go rigid. Held it. Counted. The woman counted too, her three tongue-parts making different numbers that harmonized into something wrong.

When he finished counting, the mantis returned to his mat. Put herbs on the coals that changed the smoke from gray to green to something that had no color but made your eyes water. He breathed deep but his eyes stayed clear, focused. No mystical trance. Just a man who knew his business.

When he spoke, his voice carried the weight of rehearsal.

He gave the Syracuse prophecy first. Bullshit about eagles flying backward and stone ships drowning in their own harbors.

Then he looked at me. Both eyes steady. Clear.

He said the wooden horse remembers its maker's hands. Said I was made to hold worse things than warriors. Said the horse should have kept its belly closed.

He turned to Marcus next. The empty socket fixed on him while the good eye studied his posture.

The mantis said you'll die in your brother's shadow. Said you'll spend twenty years copying his movements, trying to stand like him, walk like him, be him. Said one day in Athens you'll forget you're pretending and stand too straight in the wrong place. They'll gut you for a Spartan before you remember you're supposed to be broken. Your body will betray you by being exactly what you've practiced. The last thing you'll see is your reflection in a shield, finally standing like a citizen while your insides spill out.

Marcus's jaw worked but no sound came. That unconscious squaring of his shoulders even as the oracle promised it would kill him. His hand went to his ribs where they'd healed wrong, pressing the place that already made him stand crooked.

Then he turned to Kyrillos. The empty socket leaked faster now, pus running steady into his beard.

He said you're going to hang yourself from a kitchen beam. Said you're too human for what they've made you into. Too much iron left when they need empty vessels. Said you'll spend three years watching monsters pretend to be boys, boys becoming things that eat their own dead, and one morning you'll oil your skin with kitchen grease and kick over a crate because it's better than becoming what surrounds you.

The mantis's voice went soft. Almost gentle. Said the rope won't break your neck clean. You'll dance. Feet kicking air, looking for ground that isn't there. Your body will fight even though your mind made its choice. And these three sounds.

Behind us, the woman made noises. Her three tongue-parts working separately to create the exact sounds a crushed windpipe makes trying to breathe. Wet consonants that weren't words, just the sound of meat trying to function after function had ceased.

That's what you'll make while you dance. While your blood-brother watches because you asked him to cut you down after. Not save you. Just cut you down so you don't swing for morning count like another lesson about boys who couldn't empty themselves enough.

Kyrillos went rigid. His hand was already at his throat, fingers finding the exact spot.

The woman scratched the prophecy onto wet clay with all three tongue-parts clicking against her teeth.

The mantis said Thrasybulos already knows. Said the compound tracks everything. Which boys hear death in prophecy, which ones break toward the rope. You're already marked in his tablets. Just meat waiting to spoil.

Of course he knew. Thrasybulos had probably sent a runner ahead with our files. Three boys' weaknesses sketched in wax, delivered with silver to ensure accurate prophecies. The mantis wasn't reading our futures in smoke and blood. He was reciting intelligence reports dressed up as divine vision.

Marcus and his citizen posturing? Every instructor had seen it. Documented it. Beaten him for it.

Kyrillos already measuring beams with his eyes? Already fingering his throat when nervous? The compound tracked everything. Why wouldn't they track which boys were already rehearsing their own endings?

And me with my wooden horse prophecy. Vague enough

to mean anything, specific enough to sound profound. Classic oracle bullshit.

After, walking down the mountain, Kyrillos had stopped listening. His eyes tracked upward constantly. Checking tree branches, measuring heights, testing whether they'd hold weight. When we rested, he'd stand beneath over-hangs and reach up, seeing how far his feet would be from the ground.

The prophecy had worked perfectly. Not because the mantis could see the future, but because he'd given Kyrillos exactly the right seeds to plant. Tell a boy who's already brittle that he'll hang himself, show him exactly how it will sound, and watch him rehearse it into reality.

Marcus walked differently too. Consciously trying to slouch, to break his citizen habits. But every few steps he'd catch himself straightening. The prophecy had made him aware of his body in a way that guaranteed he'd never be able to control it.

Three days back. Marcus walked ahead, trying different postures like a man who'd discovered his own body was a trap. Kyrillos didn't speak, just measured shadows and branches. I counted the hours, wondering which of us would fulfill our prophecies first.

Once, stopping to rest where a spring cut through rock, Kyrillos asked if I remembered the first winter.

I knew he meant the frost, our backs pressed together, the only warmth either of us trusted. Before the compound taught us heat was weakness.

I said I remembered.

He nodded, cupped water in his hands, drank. That was all.

Marcus watched us from his perch on a boulder, still adjusting his stance every few breaths like he could find some position that wasn't citizen and wasn't broken. Just safe.

That night at the compound, Thrasybulos asked if I believed the prophecy. Not prophecies in general. Kyrillos's specifically.

I said prophecies were smoke and fear.

He made marks on his tablet. Deep enough to score the wood beneath. Said to watch Kyrillos. Not to prevent. Just to observe. Document. Report which beams he measured, which knots he practiced. Said the mantis had been right about the gymnasium fire. About King Archidamus dying where mountain meets sea. Said some boys' deaths were already written. The compound just needed to document how long the writing took to complete.

Right about the gymnasium fire. Right about the king. Or just well-informed about arsons planned and kings already sick. Easy to predict fires you set yourself. Easy to prophesy deaths when you have spies in every court physician's chamber.

But I nodded like I believed. Like I thought some half-blind hermit could see futures in smoke instead of just reading briefings from Thrasybulos's network. The compound wanted me to watch Kyrillos destroy himself, so I'd watch. Whether prophecy or psychology, the result would be the same.

Outside his chambers, Kyrillos waited. Asked what Thrasybulos had said.

I told him clarification about Syracuse.

He studied my face. Then nodded. But his hand was already at his throat again, fingers pressing where rope would sit.

That night in quarters, he asked if I'd cut him down when it happened. So he didn't swing for the morning count.

I said I would. The scar across my palm ached. Where the priest had cut deep enough to show yellow fat, mixed our blood with wine and salt, bound us with oaths about finishing what the other started.

Marcus sat against the far wall, still practicing postures. Broken. Citizen. Something in between that might let him live. Each position wrong in its own way.

In three years, I'd cut Kyrillos down with the same eating knife he'd asked about. In twenty, Marcus would die in Athens exactly as prophesied. And I'd survive to write this, becoming whatever a wooden horse becomes when it's fulfilled its purpose.

The compound had sent us up the mountain knowing precisely which prophecies would take root in which minds.

CHAPTER 10

THE TAX COLLECTOR

AGE 13

Three weeks had passed since the mountain prophet gave Kyrillos his death—showed him exactly how a crushed windpipe sounds trying to breathe. Three wet consonants that weren't words, just the noise meat makes when rope cuts off air. The compound had trained me to notice patterns. This one was writing itself in flesh and future fear.

Lysander gave us bronze and pointed north toward Gythium. The tax collector had been skimming silver from harbor duties, feeding ship schedules to Athens. Routine work. Should have been clean—two boys, three guards, one throat to open. But I was paired with someone whose body was already rehearsing death. His hands shook now when he wasn't holding weapons. Only bronze kept them steady.

Five years since that drunk priest had mixed our blood with wine and salt, binding us as blood-brothers in a ceremony that stank of calculation. Now I watched

Kyrillos destroy practice posts while the weight of that promise pressed against my palm. If he failed—when he failed, as the oracle had already shown—I'd answer for it. The compound hadn't created brotherhood. They'd created accountability systems where one boy's breaking would mark the other.

I rewrapped my blade handle while Kyrillos swung his mace like he was trying to beat the future out of his skull. Thinner cord, tighter wraps, the kind of adjustment you make when you know your partner might break mid-strike. Each impact harder than technique required. The posts splintered. One cracked clean through. Dion should have corrected his wild swings but just watched. Everyone could see it—Kyrillos wasn't training anymore. He was negotiating with violence, trying to find a death that wasn't rope.

Gythium stank of rotting fish and tar. The harbor district worse—sewage running in open channels, mixing with spillage from the fullers' vats. Even in winter, flies rose in clouds when you walked past. The tax collector's house sat above it all on a small rise, trying to pretend the smell didn't reach. But it did. Clung to the limestone walls, seeped through shuttered windows. Even his wife's cooking couldn't mask it, though she tried—oil crackling with garum, trying to cover decay with more decay.

We spent two days on a warehouse roof mapping his routine. Morning inspection at the harbor where he'd count cargo and take his cut. Evening wine at the Three Dolphins—always the same corner table where he could watch the door. Home by second watch. His guards played dice against the garden wall, bronze clattering on stone. The evening guard had a weakness for wine, bought it from the same vendor who worked the harbor road. The morning guard's left knee locked up in cold weather—he'd walk circles around the property to keep it loose, each circuit taking exactly two hundred breaths.

But Kyrillos had lost the careful economy that made us invisible. His walk had gone wild at the edges. The merchant guards on the Gythium road watched us pass with the wariness of men who recognized predators. When we stopped for water, he'd drink like drowning, water running down his chin. Built cook-fires too large, stared into them until his eyes reflected nothing but flame. At checkpoints, he'd meet guards' eyes until they looked away, disturbed by what they saw swimming there.

One guard—scarred veteran missing two fingers—had put his hand on his sword when Kyrillos wouldn't stop staring. I'd had to pull Kyrillos away, apologizing about my brother's head wound from the wars. The guard didn't believe it but let us pass. Everyone could smell it on us—violence looking for an excuse. But Kyrillos was looking for more than excuse. He was shopping for endings, testing each interaction to see if this stranger might be the one to give him death that wasn't the oracle's promise.

When sunset came on the second day, Kyrillos moved too early.

I was still working into position when he charged. No signal. No coordination. Just eruption. The guards hadn't finished changing shifts—three instead of two, and now they knew we were there. His mace caught the first guard's skull before the man could draw blade. Wet crack like dropped melon. Bone and brain painted the wall behind him. But the second guard was already turning, mouth opening to scream.

I had to sprint across open ground, slide my blade up under his jaw before sound could bring the garrison. The angle was bad. Caught more throat than brain stem. He dropped but kept thrashing, spraying blood in arcs while his body figured out it was dead. His heels drummed against stone. Fingernails tore grooves in the dirt. The dying always fight hardest when it's already too late.

The third guard had made it inside. Door barred now. Oil lamps flaring to life in windows. Citizens' voices rising. We'd lost every advantage.

Kyrillos kicked the door hard enough to splinter the frame but not break it. Kicked again. The wood shrieked and gave way. He charged through the gap like a man who'd forgotten spear points existed. The guard inside had good position, good stance. His thrust caught Kyrillos's shoulder, tore meat to the bone. Should have stopped him. Didn't. Kyrillos's mace crushed the guard's chest, kept swinging after the man dropped. Making paste of what had been a person. The violence had gone past purpose into argument with fate itself.

I grabbed his arm to stop him. He spun on me, eyes wild and empty at the same time. For a heartbeat I thought he'd swing on me too. Then recognition crawled back into his face like something returning from far away.

The tax collector cowered behind his strongbox, still clutching the manifest we'd come for—ship schedules, Athenian contacts, everything Lysander wanted. Ink stained his fingers where he'd been copying reports. His soft hands shook as he held out the papers, trying to buy his life with treason.

He said please. Said he had a son. Four years old. Said his name was Nikias.

The name hit different now that I knew its weight. Another helot child named for a dead rebel, another small defiance that would need pruning. But not by us. Not tonight.

I took the manifest. Opened his throat. Quick work while his son's name still hung in the air between us. Professional. What we'd come for. But Kyrillos hadn't come for professional anymore. He stood there breathing hard, blood running from his shoulder, still staring at the guard he'd turned to architecture.

The strongbox was theater. Pottery shards and river stones. A child's weight trick. The real wealth was elsewhere or never existed. And now citizens crowded outside. Garrison whistles approaching. The tax collector's wife screaming from the upper floor where Kyrillos should have been, where she should have been dead already but wasn't because he'd gone straight to violence instead of following the plan.

I threw silver pieces from the window—the few real coins mixed with the fakes. Let greed scatter the crowd for a few heartbeats. We escaped through back streets, Kyrillos leaving a blood trail any child could follow.

A mastiff found us three streets from the water. Guard dog, thick through the chest, trained to corner thieves. It came low and fast, not barking yet but growling from somewhere deep. Went for Kyrillos—probably smelled the blood, saw the weakness.

I caught it mid-leap, left hand in the loose skin of its neck, right finding the lower jaw. We hit the wall together, its weight driving air from my lungs. Hot breath and strings of spit, teeth snapping inches from my face. I hooked my thumb behind its lower teeth and pulled. The jaw separated with a wet tearing—not at the joint but through the muscle and tendon that held it closed. The dog's tongue lolled out, suddenly useless. It tried to bark but managed only a bubbling whine.

I drove my knee up into its ribs until something cracked, then pressed my boot on its neck until the thrashing stopped. Another body following the same physics. But as I stood there with dog blood mixing with the guard's on my hands, I saw Kyrillos watching. Something in his face—recognition maybe. We'd both been caught by things that wanted to tear us apart. I'd broken mine. His was still circling, waiting.

The harbor was in uproar. We stole the first boat we found—small fishing vessel, single sail, nets still wet in the bow. Slipped it past the triremes hauled up for winter maintenance, their bronze rams gleaming like teeth in the torchlight. The owner probably still drinking at the taverns, not knowing his livelihood was about to carry two killers south.

I found his personal things under the rowing bench: a wax tablet with a child's letters scratched deep (NIKIAS, over and over, practicing until he got it right), a wine cup with a chip on the rim, bronze fishhooks wrapped carefully in oiled cloth. Someone's entire life reduced to objects we'd steal without thinking. Another child learning to write that dangerous name, another small rebellion that would grow until someone like us came to prune it.

All night we sailed through black water. I worked the lines while Kyrillos bled on the tiller. The wound had opened wider—could see white of bone when he moved wrong. His good arm fought the tiller while the wounded one hung almost useless, fingers barely able to grip. He had to lean his whole body against it when the current pulled strong, steering more with his weight than his hands. Blood ran down the wood, pooling where his hip pressed against it.

The dolphins left us after the first hour. Just the slap of water on wood, the sail catching and losing wind. I found dried fish in the hold, gnawed it while watching him steer by stars he couldn't name.

I said I counted everything.

He said that's what they trained us for.

He said they trained him to die. Adjusted course, winced as the movement pulled his shoulder. Said it was just taking longer than expected.

We sailed in silence after that.

Three days later in Sparta, Lysander took our report. His eyes tracked from Kyrillos's shoulder—still seeping through rough sailcloth bandages—to the wildness that hadn't left his face. His stylus cut deep enough to score the wood beneath. He understood what I was beginning to grasp: the blood-bond hadn't created partnership. It had created a ticking mechanism where one boy's breaking would trigger consequences for both.

He told Kyrillos to wait outside. When alone, asked what had gone wrong.

I told him about the recklessness. Going too early. The violence past purpose. The unnecessary risks.

His stylus pressed deeper into wax. Said boys who knew their deaths sometimes tried to outrun them. Said the goddess collected what she was owed regardless. Just a question of how much interest accumulated before payment.

That night Kyrillos came to my quarters. Sat against my wall, knees drawn up like a child. The oil lamp burned low, making shadows dance. His fingers found his throat, pressed where rope would rest. His other hand worked at a splinter in the floorboard until it came free, left a hole he kept probing with his fingernail.

Said he saw the rope everywhere now. Every beam was measured against his height. Every cord became the one that would take him. Even closed his eyes and it was there, waiting. Asked if I'd cut him down when it happened. Neither of us believed in salvation anymore. Just cut him down after so he didn't swing for morning count.

I said I would.

He got up to leave. At the door, turned back. Said the oracle had been right about both of us. Him with his rope. Me with what I'd become. Said mine was worse.

I sat there after he left, picking hemp fibers from my blade handle. Sixteen strands, properly twisted. Strong enough to hold a man's weight. The dog's blood was still under my nails, mixed with the guard's, mixed with whatever else I'd touched that wouldn't wash clean. My hands smelled like iron and fear and that particular musk of frightened animal.

Two years before I'd keep that promise. But sitting there that night, I already knew how it would go. He'd oil his skin with kitchen grease—wrong kind, wouldn't sanctify. The drop wouldn't be enough to break his neck clean. He'd dance like the oracle promised, feet kicking air, searching for purchase that wasn't there. And I'd cut him down with the same knife I was cleaning, because promises were promises. Even blood-bonds that were really just the compound's way of ensuring mutual destruction.

We'd been trained to see patterns, predict outcomes, find breaking points. Kyrillos would hang himself not because the oracle had power, but because the oracle had shown him exactly how his throat would sound when crushed. That knowledge was the seed. Everything after was just watching it grow.

He was right about what I'd become. I could watch my blood-brother practice dying and report it to Thrasybulos with the same detachment I'd report grain counts. The compound hadn't created bonds—they'd created accountability systems dressed up as brotherhood. When Kyrillos killed himself, I'd be marked as the one who'd failed to prevent it. Another entry in their ledgers.

Later, cleaning my blade in the lamplight, I found the child's wax tablet among the fisherman's things. NIKIAS scratched over and over in clumsy letters. Same name the tax collector had gasped. Different child, same dangerous hope. I kept the tablet this time, tucked it away with other evidence of patterns worth tracking. All these little Nikiases growing up with rebellion in their names, not knowing they were marking themselves for boys like us.

The blood-bond had done exactly what the compound intended. Not created brotherhood, but ensured that when one tool broke, the other would be marked by association. I'd carry Kyrillos's failure in my record, in the scar across my palm, in the memory of watching him rehearse his own ending.

Two years later, I'd cut him down as promised. By then, I'd understand completely what that drunk priest had been doing with his blade and bowl—not joining us, but chaining us to each other's inevitable failures.

He'd asked me to cut him down because even broken tools deserve that much. To disappear clean instead of becoming education for the next batch. I'd give him that.

It wasn't brotherhood—they'd removed that years ago. Just one broken boy doing inventory on another.

CHAPTER 11

THE MOTHER

AGE 14

KYRILLOS FROZE while trying to cut a pregnant woman's throat on a morning Lysander had choreographed like a physician planning surgery. Not to execute a traitor—any fool with bronze could do that. But to confirm which boys the oracle had already broken.

A year had passed since we'd killed the tax collector in Gythium. A year of watching Kyrillos touch his throat every time he entered a room, fingers finding the exact spot where hemp would rest. His hands shook now whenever they weren't gripping bronze. The kitchen assignment after that botched mission had only given him more time to study roof beams, more quiet hours to practice those three wet sounds the oracle had taught him.

The morning they brought out Timomenes's mother, frost made the courtyard stones slick as oiled metal. I stood in formation with the others while we did this dance for the fiftieth time. But Lysander had pulled

Kyrillos from the line, positioned him at the center where everyone could watch.

The woman was maybe thirty-five. Thin everywhere except where her belly swelled with child. Eight months along. The pregnancy moved inside her when she walked —you could see it through the fabric, that alien rolling of life not yet separate. Clothes patched with whatever she could find: goat leather at the elbows, fishing net holding a tear at the hem.

They'd caught her selling garrison movements to Athens. Twelve dead at Mantinea because the enemy knew which pass we'd take. But the swollen belly made this more than execution. Made it exactly what a boy haunted by prophecy couldn't do.

She walked straight-backed between guards. No struggle —conserving everything for what came next. When she saw her son in formation, she stopped. Just one heartbeat. Her eyes traced his face like she was storing it.

Timomenes stood rigid. The cords in his jaw worked like he was chewing stones. His whole body leaned forward while training held him back.

Lysander spoke the usual words about treason and consequences. But his eyes never left Kyrillos. Measuring. Waiting.

He said the bastard inside her would die with her. Said that's what happened to traitor cunts who spread their legs for Athenian gold.

The vulgarity was deliberate. Making this about more than execution. Making it about wombs and futures and the compound's power to end both. The exact pressure to crack a boy already breaking.

He called Kyrillos forward.

Not Timomenes. That would have been the standard test —make the son execute the mother. This was about confirming how deep the oracle's rot had spread.

Kyrillos stepped into the circle. His whole body trembled now—not just hands but shoulders, neck, the small muscles around his eyes. Like something inside was dissolving.

Lysander handed him a blade. Good bronze, proper weight. I'd sharpened it the night before. Perfect edge. No excuse for what happened next.

The woman looked at her son. Not Kyrillos. Silent tears cutting through dirt on her cheeks. Her mouth moved without sound. Just shaping his name.

Then she looked at Timomenes again. Mouthed: Not your fault.

Timomenes jerked like she'd put bronze through him. Because those words meant she knew. Knew her son would carry this weight forever. Was trying to lift it before it landed.

Kyrillos raised the blade. Lowered it. Raised again. His arm shook so hard the bronze sang against itself.

I'd seen this paralysis in boys the oracle had marked. The moment when prophecy fights training and both lose.

Lysander stepped close. Said refusal meant joining her. Said the goddess demanded bronze or rope.

At rope, Kyrillos made a sound. Not words. The same three wet consonants the oracle had taught him. The exact sound a crushed windpipe makes trying to breathe. He was already there, already dancing.

Timomenes took three steps before conditioning caught him. Hand lifting toward his knife, dropping, lifting again. Frozen between son and soldier.

The woman closed her eyes. Accepting what her son couldn't.

Kyrillos went behind her. Positioned the blade. His hands shook so hard the bronze chattered. Everyone could hear his failure.

He cut.

The tremor turned it ragged. The blade caught wrong, tore instead of sliced. Blood came but not enough. Not the right vessels. She'd die slow, aware for every moment.

She made a surprised sound. Hand going to her throat where blood seeped between fingers.

Then her belly clenched. The child responding to trauma. Her water broke—clear fluid mixed with blood in the sand. Another contraction, visible through wet wool.

Timomenes screamed. Not words. Just noise from somewhere deeper than language.

He charged. Lysander's blade took him perfect—up between ribs to find heart and lung together. Economy of motion that showed why he taught and we learned.

Timomenes dropped beside his mother. She reached with her free hand. Their fingers almost touched before Lysander's boot came down on her wrist. The pressure made her belly contract again. More fluid, pink-tinged now.

I watched a body try to preserve its contents even as the container failed. Fighting to push out what might survive.

Lysander told Kyrillos to finish it.

But Kyrillos stood frozen. The woman trying to speak through blood. Timomenes working his mouth like a landed fish, pink foam where lung met air. Neither dying clean.

I took the blade from Kyrillos's hand. He didn't resist. Just stood making those three sounds against his thighs. Practicing.

I opened her throat properly. Found the arteries Kyrillos had missed. Deep enough to matter. She died looking at her son while her body still tried to push.

He died looking at her while his lungs forgot how to work.

The silence after was complete. Just wind across stone and blood finding its level. But I knew that silence—not the peaceful kind. The kind that comes before violence.

The stench of futures ended hung in morning sun—shit and birth fluid and death all mixed together.

Lysander studied Kyrillos, taking final measurements. He'd gotten his confirmation—oracle boys couldn't hold bronze steady when it mattered.

He told Kyrillos to report to the kitchens. Support work, immediately.

Kyrillos walked away without cleaning his blade. Left it there in sand mixed with things that should never mix.

That night I cleaned my knife while thinking about what we'd proven. A pregnant traitor, her son, and a boy broken by prophecy. Three deaths to confirm what Lysander already knew. Some boys heard death in prophecy and broke toward uselessness. The compound didn't try to fix them. Just sorted them into roles where shaking hands mattered less.

The compound traded in everything. Every drop of blood. Every grain of terror. Every future strangled in the womb. Even the pain we hadn't felt yet. Even the deaths we hadn't died.

In the morning, I saw Kyrillos scrubbing pots. Lye had eaten his fingertips pink. But his eyes were on the roof beams. Counting. Measuring. Testing their strength for weight they'd need to hold.

The compound had succeeded in emptying him so completely that even violence leaked out. Left him with nothing but prophecy and rope and the patience to wait for one to become the other.

Timomenes's mother had died trying to birth a future. Kyrillos would die trying to birth his prophecy. Both kinds of labor that end in blood and silence.

But I survived to write this, which means I found the balance. Empty enough to kill anyone. Full enough to keep functioning.

CHAPTER 12

THE XIPHOS

AGE 14

LOOKING BACK NOW, I finally understand what Nikandros saw that morning—the last boy who could have been Spartan instead of just Sparta's tool. He looked at Kyrillos the way you look at a good horse with a broken leg. Something that could have been magnificent, now just waiting for someone to end its misery.

But standing in formation while this one-eyed hoplite studied us like we were diseased meat, I thought he was just another instructor come to beat technique into our bodies.

Nikandros had fought at Mantinea. You could see it in how he moved—real war written in every gesture, not compound exercises. Tree-trunk arms mapped with burn scars. Left eye gone, the socket uncovered like a second mouth that spoke truths the first one wouldn't. When he walked, his weight stayed centered despite the missing eye. A man who'd learned to fight with half his vision and still lived to teach about it.

Lysander introduced him as our advanced blade instructor. Another broken specialist come to show us our futures—though I didn't understand then that Nikandros wasn't broken. He was complete in ways we'd never be.

He had us run basic drills first. Advance, thrust, withdraw. We'd done these ten thousand times. Our bodies moved without thought—sharp, clean, empty. Every movement economical, precise. No wasted energy because energy was currency and we were always bankrupt.

After an hour of watching us perform perfect technique with dead eyes, he told us to stop.

We formed up, waiting for critique. I expected the usual —better angles, deeper cuts, faster recovery.

Instead he spat in the dirt. The glob landed between his feet, deliberate as a thrown blade.

He asked if we knew what made the phalanx strong.

Theron started to answer—something about overlapping shields, mutual protection. The textbook response we'd memorized.

Nikandros cut him off with a gesture that made Theron's mouth snap shut. He said it wasn't the bronze. Wasn't the formation. It was the man beside you. His shield covering your exposed side, your shield covering his. Living and dying as one body. The phalanx wasn't just shields locked together—it was souls locked together. The gods watched men who held the line together. Athena loved those who died for their brothers.

He walked our line then, and I remember how his good eye swept over us. Quick, like looking at diseased meat you had to handle but didn't want to touch. He stopped at Kyrillos. Something in his face changed—surprise maybe, or recognition. Like finding gold in a pile of lead.

He told Kyrillos to step forward. Show his stance.

Kyrillos moved into fighting position. Even then, through all the compound's grinding, you could see it— the natural power, the way his body understood space beyond just his own survival. His hips squared to cover angles that would protect a man on his left. His shield arm positioned not for solo defense but for overlapping coverage. Seven years in this place and his body still remembered what brotherhood looked like.

Nikandros circled him slowly. Told him to thrust.

Kyrillos did—perfect form, economy of motion, weight behind it without overcommitting. But more than that. His recovery brought his shield back to cover that empty space where a brother should have been standing. The phantom protection of someone trained for the line.

Nikandros's voice went soft then. Dangerous soft. He said Kyrillos had the body of a hoplite. The instincts. The soul for it. Said in the phalanx line, his brothers would trust him to hold. Would sing his name at the syssitia when he fell defending the man beside him. The gods would know him. Would welcome him as a man who understood what mattered.

Then his voice turned hard as the bronze we carried. He said instead, Kyrillos was here with these fucking snakes. Boys who'd step on each other's throats for an extra barley cake. Who'd sell each other's position for a warmer spot to sleep. Said no god watched boys like us. We were pollution walking. Miasma in human form.

He had us pair for shield work. Told us to fight as brothers would—protect each other while attacking another pair. Show him the phalanx in miniature. The pairing revealed everything.

Kyrillos paired with Marcus. When they locked shields, something almost worked. Kyrillos moved to cover Marcus's weak side without being told. When Marcus stumbled on the uneven stones, Kyrillos steadied him with his shield arm while maintaining guard. His body knew the dance even if his mind was already elsewhere.

But Marcus didn't reciprocate. When Kyrillos pressed forward, Marcus hung back, preserving his own position. When the other pair flanked, Marcus stepped away instead of turning with his partner. Not from cowardice —from seven years of learning that self-preservation was the only preservation that mattered.

Nikandros stopped them. Asked Marcus why he'd abandoned his brother.

Marcus looked confused. Like the question was in a language he'd never learned. He said he wasn't abandoning anyone. Just maintaining position. Following the drills. Seven years of conditioning speaking through his mouth.

And he was right. We'd learned to maintain position. To preserve ourselves. To trust only in our own blade, our own shield, our own ability to survive. Everything else was someone else's problem.

Nikandros moved faster than a one-eyed man should. Grabbed Marcus by the shoulders—hands still carrying heat from real forges, not our practice ones. His grip found the exact points where a hoplite instructor would hold a student, fingers pressing into the muscles that should know brotherhood.

He forced Marcus into position beside Kyrillos. Hip to hip, shields overlapping. His hands tried to teach what years of drills should have beaten into Marcus's body—the slight forward lean that said you trusted the man beside you, the angle that protected your partner's exposed side.

But the moment Nikandros let go, Marcus's body slid back to solo stance like water finding its level. Weight back on his heels. Shield pulling inward. The compound's programming rejecting brotherhood at the muscular level.

Nikandros tried again. Harder this time, his frustration making his scarred hands shake. Forced Marcus forward, positioned his shield arm, even kicked his feet into the proper stance. Held him there while we all watched.

Let go. Marcus reverted instantly. His body couldn't hold the position any more than water could flow uphill.

He tried with Dimitri next. Same result. Then Philippos. Each boy's muscles sliding back to self-preservation the moment his hands released them. I watched him realize what we were—not poorly trained but trained wrong at the cellular level. Boys whose bodies had been programmed to reject the very thing that made the phalanx work.

The smell of his sweat filled the training yard—different from ours. Real war-sweat, carrying the memory of actual battles where men died for each other. We just smelled like fear and survival.

When he'd tried to position six of us and watched six bodies reject brotherhood like a transplanted organ, he stepped back. His good eye tracked along our faces while the empty socket wept.

Then he grabbed Kyrillos's shoulder—I saw his fingers find the exact spot where the straps from the long walk had left their channels. Kyrillos flinched, not from pain but from memory. Nikandros said this one understood brotherhood. Had the soul for it. Could feel it in how his muscles moved. But he was trapped here with boys who'd been trained to refuse what he still remembered. Boys who could form a line but would never hold one. Who could stand together but would never fall together.

He walked our line again, spitting after every third boy. When he stopped between me and Philippos, he told us to lock shields. We did—perfect overlap.

Then he drove his weight between us.

We split like rotted wood. No resistance. No instinct to brace together. When his shoulder hit the point where our shields met, my body stepped left while Philippos went right. Seven years of compound training had made self-preservation our only instinct—mutual defense simply wasn't there. Like asking your right hand to protect your left while someone cut it off. The body doesn't work that way. Neither did we.

He called us cattle. Worse than cattle. At least cattle moved as a herd. We were bodies that happened to be standing near other bodies. I understood then what he was really showing us—not poor technique but fundamental absence. We couldn't even comprehend what was missing.

When he paired us for blade work, he put Kyrillos with Dimitri. Told them to protect each other while sparring another pair. Show him brotherhood with bronze.

Kyrillos tried. When Dimitri overextended chasing an opening, Kyrillos covered. When the other pair pressed, Kyrillos stepped forward to shield him. His body flowing through movements it had never been taught but somehow knew.

But Dimitri fought alone. Used Kyrillos's protection without thought of returning it. When Kyrillos needed cover, Dimitri was pursuing his own attack. When Kyrillos took a hit meant for both of them, Dimitri didn't even notice.

Nikandros stopped them. The look he gave Kyrillos—I'd later recognize it in Athens when I saw mothers watching their sons march to wars they wouldn't return from. Not pity exactly. Grief for something that hadn't died yet but would.

He said the tragedy wasn't that we were monsters. Monsters had purpose. The tragedy was boys like Kyrillos—still human enough to remember brotherhood but trapped with things that had forgotten. Still pure enough for the gods to see but surrounded by miasma that would drag him down. The soul of a hoplite wasted on boys who'd never understand what they were watching die.

That night I overheard Nikandros speaking to Lysander in the weapons storage. Years of training had made us ghosts who could hear through stone, read lips in darkness. They thought we couldn't hear.

Nikandros said one boy might have made the line. The big one who still carried himself like a soldier. Still had iron in him instead of the nothing he saw in the rest of us. Still understood what it meant to stand beside another man. But not here. Not with these others. Like trying to forge hoplites from helot dogs. The one boy who could have been something was surrounded by boys who'd drag him down to their level. Or lower.

By day's end, Nikandros had gone quiet. When he gathered us for final words, the disgust had curdled into something else. The sun bled out behind the western peaks as he spoke.

He said tomorrow he'd teach us the xiphos because duty demanded it. Because Lysander had asked. Because even pollution needed to know how to hold bronze properly. But we'd never understand why Spartans carried them. The xiphos was the brotherhood blade. When your spear broke, your brothers' swords protected you. When you fell, they stood over you. The bronze itself carried prayers, blessed by priests who understood what men owed each other.

He looked at Kyrillos one last time. That same look— grief for the living. He said in another life, men would have called him shield-brother. Would have shared wine at the same fire. Would have poured libations when he fell holding the line. The young men would have learned his story. How the gods welcomed him.

Instead he was here. With us. Snakes wearing bronze. The goddess had marked us for different purposes. Not to hold lines but to slip through them. Not to die with brothers but to die alone, unmourned, our names forgotten before our ashes cooled.

That night in quarters, Kyrillos sat apart. Not unusual— we all sat apart. But his isolation felt different now. Heavier.

Philippos asked what Nikandros had meant about the songs. About names in temples.

Kyrillos said it didn't matter. The syssitia sang for men who fell beside their brothers. Not for boys marked by oracles. Not for tools that broke before they could be used properly.

I watched him count the roof beams in our quarters. Testing heights with his eyes. Already knowing he'd never stand in the line Nikandros had seen in him. Never be the hoplite worth remembering at fires, worth teaching young men about. Just another broken tool burning with the week's failures.

I see what Nikandros was really doing. Not teaching us the xiphos—we already knew how to use blades. He was sorting us one last time. Separating tools from the one boy who might have been human. Confirming what the compound already knew: Kyrillos would break because he still had something in him worth breaking. The rest of us would survive because we were already broken in all the ways that mattered.

That's what made us perfect for the work ahead. Not strong—broken in exactly the right places. Like bronze with deliberate weak points that would bend but not shatter. Kyrillos was the flaw in the batch. Too much iron left. Too much memory of what boys were supposed to become.

The compound would fix that. The oracle had already shown him how.

Nikandros had come to teach us about brotherhood. Instead he'd taught us we were incapable of it. All except one. And that one would die rather than live surrounded by what we'd become.

The xiphos was the brotherhood blade.

We were just the things that carried them.

CHAPTER 13

THE HARVEST

LYSANDER GAVE us black cloaks and bronze. Four sectors to clear. Helots stealing grain, breeding rebellion in their children's names. Me, Kyrillos, Marcus, and Silas who'd been caught with kitchen stores in his mat. Provincial work—the last chance for boys on the edge of breaking.

I knew why Lysander paired me with Kyrillos. Not partnership. Observation. Document how deep the oracle's rot had spread since that pregnant woman's blood had painted the courtyard. Since Nikandros had seen something human in him that needed grinding out. The compound was always watching its investments, calculating when to cut losses.

New moon. The barley reached our chests, heavy with stolen grain. We spread through it twenty paces apart, black shapes in black night. The grain whispered against our cloaks like dying breaths. Somewhere, a dog started barking. They always knew first—smelled what we were before we arrived. Then the barking cut short. Even dogs learned not to announce us.

Marcus found the trail. Six or seven bodies pushing east through the grain. One dragged a bad leg—every fourth stalk bent lower where the limb had scraped. Fresh enough the grain still tried to straighten. The drag pattern said old injury, maybe Provincial work that hadn't quite killed him. Those were the dangerous ones. Survivors who knew our patterns.

Silas pressed his ear to the ground, counting movements through earth. He'd been dying slowly since the second winter, when he learned that stone carries sound and sound carries death. I'd found him that morning with his ear frozen to the barracks wall, trying to hear Theron strangle the hoarder two rooms away. Had to pour piss from the bucket to separate skin from stone. Left a pink patch on the granite and a raw wound on his ear that wept constantly. Now he heard violence gathering every-where—in footsteps, in breathing, in the way bodies displaced air.

He pointed us toward the threshing circle before we could see it. Said seven heartbeats moving wrong. Said one was small. Too small.

The threshing circle was ancient. Stone floor worn smooth by generations separating wheat from chaff. The irony wasn't lost—we were here to separate too. A boy watched from the grinding stone—maybe thirteen, trying to look brave. His bladder had already betrayed him. Dark stain spreading down his tunic. Below, five men and three women loaded grain sacks. Fast. Practiced. They knew the dance because their parents had danced it, and their parents before them.

The woman had a baby strapped to her back. Six months old, maybe seven. It made small sounds while she worked —not crying, just those soft noises babies make when they're trying to understand the world. Dark hair. Dark eyes. The kind of child that would grow up to ask questions if we let it.

We took positions. North, south, east, west. The compound had taught us to work like this—inevitable as weather, efficient as plague. Marcus moved on the lookout first. Hand over mouth, blade through kidney. The boy's legs kicked twice, trying to run horizontal. His bladder had been empty but his bowels weren't. The smell mixed with barley dust and fear-sweat.

The big man looked up at the sound—soft thud of knees hitting stone. He whistled—three short, one long. Warning pattern. They scattered like they'd practiced. But we'd practiced longer.

I caught the one with the bad leg in ten strides. Hamstring first—blade through the meat of it. The sound like cutting wet rope. He pitched forward, tried to crawl. I followed him down, found the gap between his third and fourth vertebrae. The specific spot Dionysios had shown us. Slid the blade in, twisted. His legs stopped working instantly but his mouth kept moving. Trying to warn the others even as his body shut down in sections.

Behind me, someone screamed. Cut short. Then wet choking. Silas's work—he'd learned to find throats by sound alone.

A woman crawled through the grain, leg dragging. The severed hamstring meant she wasn't going far. Silas had heard her first—pointed her out with that ruined ear of his, reading her panicked heartbeat through stem and soil. She kept crawling anyway, fingers clawing earth, even though we both knew the arithmetic. Ten yards. Twenty. Blood trail marking her path like paint.

I opened her throat. Cut through the scream before it could form. But what I remember is that she kept crawling for three more pulls. Body not accepting what the mind must have known. That's what people do— they keep trying even after the outcome is decided. Hope is just another muscle that takes time to stop twitching.

At the circle, Kyrillos had the woman with the baby backed against the threshing stone. Five paces between them. His blade still clean. This was the test Lysander had arranged. Could the boy who'd frozen on a pregnant woman kill a mother with an infant watching?

She talked fast. Messenian dialect. The words came out jumbled—the baby was innocent. Named Nikias. Another small rebellion in a name. Father dead in the quarries. She could leave him at the village gates.

Someone would find him. Raise him. He didn't have to die for grain.

The baby worked one arm free from the wrapping. Reached for Kyrillos. Not understanding. Just seeing something interesting. Dark eyes, almost black. Same shape as its mother's but without the fear yet. That pure curiosity that doesn't know to be afraid.

Kyrillos's blade shook. I could see the tremor from twenty paces. The same shake that had made him fail with Timomenes's mother. The oracle's prophecy working through his muscles, making him weak where we needed sharp.

Marcus came from the grain, blade wet to the hilt. Started toward her. Moving to finish what Kyrillos couldn't.

Kyrillos told him to check the eastern paths. Voice cracking on the words.

Marcus looked at him. At me. I nodded. Let this play out. Let Lysander get his answer about which boys could empty themselves completely. Marcus left, but I saw him glance back. We all knew what was happening. Another tool discovering its limitations.

The woman kept talking. How the baby smiled. How he reached for sunlight. How he'd grow strong. Good hands for working. Never cause trouble. Never ask questions. Never need removing.

Lies wrapped in a mother's desperation. That baby named Nikias would grow up knowing his heritage. Would ask why Spartans owned what Messenia had built. Would marry some girl who remembered the old songs. Would breed more questions in more children. The compound had taught us to see these patterns. To prune futures before they could flower.

Kyrillos lowered his blade.

Told her to run.

She ran. Clutching that baby tight, grain stalks whipping behind her. I counted ten paces. Gave her that much hope. Then put my blade through her spine at the L3 vertebra. The spot that drops them conscious but paralyzed. She needed to see what came next.

She twisted as she fell, tried to land so the baby wouldn't be crushed. Mother instinct outlasting motor function. Landed on her back. Still breathing, pink foam on her lips from a nicked lung. Eyes moving between me and her child. Understanding flooding through them.

The baby screamed. High and thin. The sound they make when they know something's wrong but not what. Its mother tried to speak but only blood came out. Tried to reach for it but her arms wouldn't work.

Kyrillos made a sound—not words. Just noise from his throat. The same wet consonants the oracle had taught him. He was already practicing, already there.

I knelt beside her. Let her see the blade. Let her understand. Then opened her throat properly. Ear to ear. The kind of cut that sprays. Got some in my mouth—copper and salt and whatever fear tastes like. She died watching me wipe her blood from the baby's face with steady hands.

The baby kept screaming. Reaching for its mother whose eyes had gone empty. Reaching for Kyrillos like he was supposed to fix this.

Kyrillos said it would die slow. Animals. Exposure. Said it without looking at me. Without looking at anything.

Silas emerged from the grain, ear cocked. Said it wasn't our problem. Said garrison patrols were two valleys over. Said we had six more bodies to find before dawn. Already moving to the next violence while this one was still warm.

The baby reached for Kyrillos again. Blood on its face making it look newborn. Its mother's blood. Black hair matted with what had sprayed. Still making those sounds —confused, scared, but not understanding why its world had gone wrong. Just knowing it had.

I studied it. Six months old. Maybe seven. Already reaching for things. Already trying to engage with the world. Another year and it would be walking. Two years, talking. Three years, asking questions. The same questions its mother had asked. The same questions her mother had asked. Generations of questions we were paid to silence.

The efficient thing was a blade through the soft spot. Quick. Clean. Add it to the tally. But Kyrillos was watching now, and this was his test. Let him see what the compound required. Let him understand that Provincial work meant killing everything that might grow into a problem. Every future. Every question. Every reaching hand.

I picked up the baby. It weighed nothing. Bird bones and soft flesh. It stopped crying, confused by the change. Looked at me with those dark eyes. Its mother's eyes without the fear. Without the understanding of what I was.

Kyrillos walked into the grain. Couldn't watch. Couldn't do it himself. Couldn't stop me. Just removed himself from the arithmetic.

I set the baby back on its mother's corpse. Let it find her breast by instinct. Let it try to nurse from the dead. It would die slower this way—exposure, dehydration, maybe animals. But it would die with its mouth on its mother's breast, trying to draw milk from meat going cold. The cruelty of that specific hope seemed important. Let the morning patrol find that tableau. Let them understand what happened to breeders of questions.

We found Kyrillos in the olive grove, vomiting. Two helots down but messy. One had crawled thirty paces dragging his guts like rope. The other took three cuts to die—arms, belly, finally throat. Like Kyrillos had forgotten where the kill spots were. Or like he was trying to make the violence matter through volume rather than precision. Amateur work from hands that had been professional three months ago.

I told Marcus to finish the sweep. Took Kyrillos aside. His hands shook worse now. The tremor running up through his shoulders.

He said the baby had reached like his brother. Before the fever took him. Same weight in the arms. Same trust.

I said the compound didn't pay us to weigh babies against memory.

He said he knew that. Said he knew exactly what the compound paid us for. Said that was the problem.

Second night. Vineyards near Therapne. Seven dead including two boys making their first wine. Maybe twelve years old. They'd fought with pruning knives, died badly. Kyrillos killed two but mechanical, empty. Going through the motions of violence without the purpose that made it clean. His cuts were getting worse. Hesitation marks. Multiple wounds where one would have worked.

Third night. Cache behind thornbush. Twenty sacks of grain. Three guards. The men fought hard—one got his teeth into Marcus's forearm before Silas opened his throat. The old woman just worked her prayer beads while I cut her throat. Olive pits strung on sinew. Her fingers kept moving after. Three more pits. Four. Muscle memory outlasting consciousness. Then nothing.

We burned it all. Let the smoke tell other villages what happened to hoarders.

Back at the compound. Lysander took our count. Thirteen confirmed dead. Plus the baby left to die on its mother's corpse—I didn't count that one. Wasn't sure how to mark it. Death by hope seemed outside our usual tallies.

Lysander watched Kyrillos during the debrief. Made marks in his tablet. Deep enough to score the wood. We all knew what those marks meant. Boy who couldn't kill babies couldn't do Provincial work. Boy who vomited at necessary violence was worse than useless. Was liability.

That afternoon, poison training. The Egyptian demonstrated extraction from cherry pits. Concentrated enough, it mimicked a wasting disease. Kyrillos's hands shook too much to grind properly. Spilled half the extraction. The Egyptian struck him. Not teaching violence—dismissal violence. The kind that said you weren't worth proper correction anymore.

Lysander pulled him aside. Reassigned to kitchens. Permanent support duty.

That night Kyrillos sat against my wall. First time since the tax collector. First time since his shoulder had healed but his mind hadn't.

He said the baby had reached for him. Said it had his brother's weight. The one who died of fever at two. Same small hands. Same trust that someone would help.

He stood to leave. At the door, turned back. Said weapons don't remember. Said that's what made us useful. Then said he'd discovered he wasn't a weapon anymore. Just a boy who remembered too much.

Next morning, kitchens. He scrubbed pots while lye ate his fingertips pink. But his eyes were on the roof beams. Measuring. Always measuring.

The harvest had sorted us. Who could kill men. Who could kill women. Who could kill tomorrow itself. A baby reaching for help was just another future that needed ending. Most of us learned that arithmetic. Could perform the necessary violence on anything that might grow into questions.

Kyrillos couldn't. That reaching hand had found something in him that hadn't been emptied. Some vestige of what Nikandros had seen. Within two years, hemp rope and roof beam. But he was already dead when that baby reached for him. Already gone when he couldn't make himself end that small rebellion before it could grow.

Later, in Athens, I'd count the children I'd removed. Three hundred? Four? The number blurred because they weren't really children to me. Just future problems requiring present solutions. Just questions that would never be asked.

But I remember that baby's weight. Remember setting it on its dead mother to nurse from nothing. Remember thinking the cruelty of that specific hope was important.

That dying while trying to draw milk from the dead was its own lesson.

That's what Provincial work taught. Not just killing. Killing everything. Every future. Every question. Every reaching hand that might grow into something requiring removal.

Even tomorrow reaching for you with baby hands and mother's eyes.

Especially that.

CHAPTER 14

THE AGOGE

THEY SENT us to collect a citizen's son who'd gotten his skull caved in during agoge training. Not just disposal work—Lysander was holding up a mirror to show us exactly what they'd removed from us.

The agoge detail wasn't about the corpse work—any helot could have scraped brains off stone. Lysander wanted us to see real Spartan training, to understand what we weren't and never would be. Like showing a gelding stallions at work. Here's what you'll never have. Here's what they emptied from you to make room for other purposes.

Four of us in that work party: me, Marcus, Philippos, and Kyrillos still serving kitchen duty. Dawn work, when citizens wouldn't see us handling their dead. Lysander gave us the cart and tools like we were collecting any other broken equipment. Hemp sacks for the body, lime for the blood, the practiced efficiency of making death disappear.

The Platanista sat between two rivers where the agoge boys beat each other into citizens. Different from our compound cut into mountain stone—this was open ground, visible, part of the city's pride. Their boys weren't hidden away like shameful necessities. They trained where fathers could watch sons become what fathers had been.

We found him by the plane trees, this citizen's boy who'd paid the price for belonging. Fifteen years old, fed and trained properly—not our meager rations. Left side of his skull pushed in where something—fist, foot, stone— had found the weak spot. The blood under him had already gone thick, drawing flies in the morning warmth. Training accident, they'd call it. The kind that reminded the rest what standards meant.

Marcus and I loaded the body while Philippos spread lime. Kyrillos was supposed to be helping but stood frozen, watching across the water where agoge boys were arriving for morning drill.

The agoge instructor looked like what we were supposed to become. Thirty-five, maybe forty. Both eyes intact, no visible scarring, the kind of complete body that spoke of careful violence rather than our grinding consumption. He had them running laps while singing—some shit about bronze and fathers and glory. Their voices carried across the water, strong and sure and together.

When they finished, he called one forward. Skinny kid, slower than the rest, the kind of weakness that in our compound would have meant kitchen work or feeding crows. The instructor asked the group what happened to boys who embarrassed their unit.

They answered together: They learn. Twenty voices making one sound.

He told them to show the weak one how to learn.

The boys circled their weak member without hesitation. The first punch folded him—solar plexus, good placement. He went down gasping. They kicked him while he was down, but organized. Taking turns. Kidney shots, thigh strikes, nothing that would cripple. Everything that would hurt. The beating was methodical as a blade drill.

But when the instructor called stop, they stopped instantly. Then they picked him up. Two boys steadied him while another checked his ribs with careful fingers. Someone produced water. The boy who'd thrown the first punch leaned in, whispered something that made the beaten boy nod and almost smile through split lips.

They made space for him in formation. Adjusted their lines so he could stand despite what had to be broken ribs. When they moved to spear drills, they covered his weak side without being told.

Beside me, Marcus had gone rigid. His knuckles white on the cart handle. The boy who'd checked the beaten kid's ribs—same nose as Marcus, same way of standing with weight back. His brother, the one who'd gone to different training because their father had status. The one who got to learn about brotherhood while Marcus learned how to survive alone.

Philippos said we had work to do. But his voice was wrong. We all heard what we were seeing. These boys beat each other to make the group stronger. We beat each other to establish who would eat.

While we scraped citizen brain matter off stone, the agoge boys locked shields. The phalanx formation Nikandros had shown us, but different when boys who trusted each other performed it. Their shields overlapped perfect, each boy's protection extending to his neighbor. When one stumbled, the line adjusted without breaking. When the instructor tested their formation with his staff, they braced together, pushed back as one body.

The beaten boy held his position despite ribs that must have screamed. The others had slowed their advance pace so he could match it. Not ordered to—just did it. Like breathing. Like knowing that the line was only as strong as its weakest shield, so you made that shield stronger instead of discarding it.

I understood then what Nikandros had seen when he tested us. Why he'd called us snakes and pollution. We could form the same shapes, perform the same movements, but something essential was missing. These agoge boys would die for each other because they'd been raised to see themselves in each other. We'd been emptied of that recognition, taught that other boys were just competition for resources, future corpses who might die before us if we were smart enough.

Marcus's brother called something to the beaten boy— encouragement maybe, or instruction. The beaten boy straightened despite the pain, found some reservoir of strength in his brothers' presence. They'd hurt him to teach him, then lifted him to show he belonged even hurt. The violence had been love filtered through Spartan logic.

We loaded our corpse while they trained. This citizen's boy who'd died reaching for what those others had. His skull had given way during some drill, some test, some moment when being almost good enough wasn't enough. But he'd died among brothers who'd remember his name, speak it at their syssitia, tell stories of how he'd tried. Not like us, dying alone in mountain snow or hanging from kitchen beams, remembered only as cautionary tales about what happened to broken tools.

Philippos told us to move. We had the body loaded, the blood limed, the evidence of failure erased. Time to go before citizens arrived and saw us near their sons.

As we left, the agoge boys were practicing spear techniques. The beaten one struggled with the movements, ribs making each thrust agony. Without discussion, two others positioned themselves beside him, demonstrated the modified stance that would hurt less. He copied them, found he could function despite the damage.

That's what broke something in me. Not the beating—I'd seen and done worse. But the automatic brotherhood, the assumption that damaged members got fixed, not discarded. These boys were being shaped into men who'd hold the line at Thermopylae. We were being shaped into things that slipped through lines to open throats in darkness.

Marcus hadn't spoken since seeing his brother. He pushed the cart mechanical, eyes fixed ahead, but I could see his jaw working. Chewing on the reality that while he'd been learning to hoard bread and count exits, his brother had been learning to trust others with his life. Two sons, same father, sorted into different machines before they knew machines existed.

At the burning ground, the priests took our delivery without questions. They knew compound boys bringing bodies meant no questions. While the pyre consumed evidence of failed citizenship, Kyrillos said quiet that they'd beaten him together but picked him up after.

Marcus said we do the same thing.

Kyrillos shook his head. Said they picked him up after.

Nobody answered that. What was there to say? That weakness meant opportunity? That every boy who broke meant more food for survivors? That we stepped on the fallen, not lifted them?

The smoke rose black against morning sky. Somewhere behind us, the agoge boys would be finishing their drills. Going home to fathers who'd teach them more about being citizens. Eating meals they didn't have to fight for. Sleeping without checking if their bunkmate might strangle them for an extra ration.

That night I dreamed about the formation. Not ours—we'd lost the ability to dream of belonging. But theirs. Shields locked, brothers beside brothers, the beaten boy held up by group strength. Moving forward together even limping.

I woke to Kyrillos screaming. Another prophecy dream. Marcus sat against his wall, staring at nothing, probably seeing his brother's hands checking ribs with the careful touch of someone who knew hurt could be fixed.

This is what Lysander had wanted us to see. Not how citizens trained—we'd never be citizens. But the shape of what we were missing. The compound hadn't just taught us violence. It had removed our capacity for brotherhood the same way it taught us to remove organs. Showed us where connection should live, then replaced it with function.

Those agoge boys beating their weakest member weren't just teaching him to be stronger. They were affirming he belonged enough to be worth beating. That investment of violence as education rather than elimination—that was citizenship being forged.

We were never meant for that forge. We were the other thing Sparta needed. The ones who could kill without brothers to mourn us, without names worth remembering, without the web of connection that makes men hesitate. They'd emptied us of everything that would have let us lock shields with another human being.

The agoge made citizens. The compound made us. Both necessary. Both violent. Only one human.

The pure fucking cruelty of that morning was making us clean up after failed citizenship while watching successful citizenship train. Like forcing a gelding to watch stallions mount mares. Here's what you can never be. Now get back to being what we cut you down to.

Marcus never mentioned his brother again. But sometimes during shield drills, I'd catch him trying to position himself to cover another boy's weak side. The movement would start, then abort, his body remembering it had been programmed for solitary survival. You could see the exact moment when instinct met compound training and lost.

That's what they'd done to us. Removed not just softness or weakness but the very ability to see ourselves in others. The agoge boys had beaten their brother to teach him. We'd have beaten him to take his rations. Same violence, different purpose. Different product.

Both Spartan. Only one worth songs.

That citizen boy's corpse weighed more than the helots we'd practiced on—better fed, more muscle. But also the weight of what he represented. A failed attempt at belonging to something we'd never be part of. He'd died trying to become what those other boys already were. We lived because that possibility had been removed before we knew to miss it.

CHAPTER 15

THE ROPE

TWO YEARS after the oracle showed Kyrillos exactly what sound a crushed windpipe makes trying to breathe, I found him in the kitchens at his usual station. Dawn hadn't broken yet. He was scrubbing the same bronze pot he'd been cleaning for twenty minutes, hands working mechanical while his eyes measured roof beams.

The lye had eaten through his fingertips until pink flesh showed through. Some boys' hands hardened to it. His just kept dissolving, layer by layer, like the compound was erasing him from the outside in. He didn't notice me until I spoke.

I told him I needed whetstones from equipment storage. The shared stones were worn to nothing from boys learning angles wrong. Advanced students got access to the good ones locked away. Part of proving you could be trusted with maintaining your own edge.

He said storage would be locked until after first count. Always was. Proper protocol. His voice came out flat, like it was traveling from somewhere distant.

I showed him the bronze key Lysander had given me the week before. Said advanced students got different protocols.

His hands stopped moving in the wash water but stayed submerged. Pink threads of blood clouded around them where the lye had gone too deep. He said he used to be good at sharpening blades. Back when he was still real— that's how he said it, like he'd already become a ghost and was just waiting for his body to notice. Said each blade wanted a different angle, different pressure. You had to listen to what the metal was telling you.

His eyes went to the beam above the pot-washing station. Measuring again. Always measuring. The beam was solid oak, thick as a man's thigh. Could hold three times his weight without creaking.

Then he asked if I remembered the oracle. The mantis with his weeping eye and prophecies that planted themselves in boys' heads like seeds in shit.

I said I remembered.

He said the oracle had been wrong about one thing. Said when the rope takes your air, you don't dance. You fight. Your body fights even when your mind has already accepted what's happening. You claw at the rope, kick at nothing, try to climb air itself. The meat wants to live even when you've decided it shouldn't.

He pulled his hands from the water. The fingertips were gone down to the first joint on three fingers. Just exposed meat that wouldn't stop bleeding. He studied them like they belonged to someone else.

He said he'd been practicing the knots. Hemp rope, properly twisted. Sixteen strands. Strong enough to hold without stretching. The running bowline was best—slides tight, doesn't loosen when weight shifts. He'd measured the drop. Three hands from beam to floor with the crate kicked over. Not enough to break the neck. He'd strangle slow, conscious for all of it.

He asked if I still carried my eating knife. The one I'd had since first year.

I touched where it hung at my belt. Standard issue but mine had good balance, held an edge. Asked why he wanted to know.

He said when it happened, he'd need someone to cut him down after. Didn't want to hang there for morning count like a lesson. Everyone staring. Making jokes about dancing lessons finally working out. The compound would use his body as education—this is what happens to boys who let oracles inside their heads. This is what happens when you can't empty yourself enough.

He wanted to just be gone. Disappear into smoke like we all would eventually. But clean. Not as a teaching tool.

Then, quieter, he said I was the only one who'd do it right. Cut clean. Not saw through like some would, making it worse. Not leave me there to prove something. Just cut and carry and burn. Inventory work.

I told him I'd cut him down.

He nodded, went back to scrubbing. The pot was already clean but his hands needed something to do. Blood kept threading through the water. Before I left, he said tomorrow morning. Before first count. Equipment storage had good beams and would be empty. He'd oil his skin but not with the sacred oils. Kitchen grease was all he had access to. Wrong kind for temple business. The goddess would refuse him. Mountain fire, not proper cremation.

He said he'd figured out those three words the oracle had spoken. Not old Greek or mountain dialect. Just sounds. The exact sounds your throat makes when the rope crushes your windpipe and you're trying to breathe through collapsed passages. Wet consonants that weren't words, just the noise of meat trying to function after function has been cut off. He'd been practicing them for two years. Now he wanted to hear if the oracle had gotten them right.

I left him there. Should have stayed. Should have done something. But the compound had trained us that weakness was individual. That broken tools were responsible for their own disposal. That interference was just delaying the inevitable.

That night I sharpened my eating knife. Not because it needed it. Because my hands needed something to do while I waited for morning. The whetstone sang against the blade. Perfect pitch when the angle was right. I thought about Kyrillos saying blades wanted different things. About listening to what the metal was telling you. This blade had been telling me for years that it was made for cutting. Tonight it would cut hemp instead of meat. Same physics. Different inventory.

Dawn came gray through the barracks window. I waited for the sound of discovery—shouts, running feet, the chaos of a body found. Nothing. Just the normal sounds of the compound waking. Morning count approaching.

I went to equipment storage.

The door stood open when it should have been locked.

The smell hit first—shit and piss but also the rancid kitchen grease he'd used to oil his skin. Wrong ritual for wrong reasons. He'd prepared with the same methodical care we brought to everything, but missed the fundamental point. You can't sanctify your own ending. The goddess turns away from self-murder, no matter how carefully you prepare the body.

He hung from the beam he'd been measuring for months. Faced the door, body twisted from the rope's rotation during the struggle. The running bowline had slipped during the thrashing, shifted sideways on his neck. Made the strangling take longer. His face had gone purple-black from blood that couldn't drain. Tongue dark and swollen, caught between teeth he'd bitten through. The whites of his eyes were solid red from burst vessels.

But it was his feet that told the real story. Scraped arcs in the dust where they'd searched for the crate he'd kicked over. The pattern showed how long he'd fought. Not dancing—the oracle had been wrong about that. Desperate scrabbling. Animal panic. The body's argument with the mind's decision. Grooves in the dust that said even prepared death was uglier than expected.

His fingers were torn where he'd clawed at the rope. Ripped the nails off trying to get purchase on the hemp. The running bowline had tightened beyond any release. His body had fought even after his mind must have known it was over. That's what the oracle hadn't mentioned—how the meat rebels against its own ending.

I counted how long he'd been hanging. Body still warm to touch when I checked for the pulse that wasn't there. Still settling into death's positions. Maybe an hour since he'd kicked the crate. Maybe less. Early enough that rigor hadn't started. Late enough that everything had voided. The smell of shit and piss and kitchen grease and that particular stink of terrorized meat.

Footsteps in the corridor. Morning patrol making rounds.

I got the ladder from the corner, climbed up beside him. The smell was worse up close—grease and death and prophecy fulfilled. His body had twisted during the struggle, and I had to turn him to reach the rope. His skin was slick with the kitchen grease. Wrong texture. Like handling raw meat that had been left in the sun.

Cut the rope with my eating knife. The blade Kyrillos had asked about. The hemp parted clean—sixteen strands, properly twisted, just like he'd said. Strong enough to hold a man's weight through all that thrashing.

He dropped wet, hit the floor like a sack of grain. The impact pushed out the last air that wasn't really breath anymore, just physics working on dead meat. His body made those three sounds then—the exact wet consonants the oracle had demonstrated. Air forcing through the crushed windpipe. Prophecy confirmed in the dropping.

Two guards arrived as I arranged him on the floor. Veterans who'd found hanging boys before. One went to report while the other helped me search for the note they always left.

Found it in his tunic—torn parchment with charcoal words: He heard me.

Not what I'd expected. Not about dancing or oracles or the compound grinding him down to nothing. Just acknowledgment that someone had heard those three sounds he'd been practicing. That someone had understood what he was trying to perfect. That the oracle's prophecy had been accurate down to the consonant.

I pocketed it before the guard could see. Some prophecies didn't need to be recorded in the official tablets.

We carried him to the preparation room where the priest was already working on another failure. Boy who'd drunk hemlock rather than face morning blade work. Poor choice—hemlock takes too long, gives you too much time to think about what you've done. The priest had him opened on the table, examining organs for signs the poison could have been survived with proper treatment. Making notes about which boys chose which endings, looking for patterns in the self-disposal.

When he saw Kyrillos, the priest made that wet clicking sound with his tongue that meant disgust. Not at the death—at the method. Self-murder offended the gods. Worse, he'd done it wrong. Used kitchen grease instead of sacred oils. Faced the door instead of the altar direction. Chose hemp over bronze. Everything about it was backwards, profane.

The priest pressed the distended tongue back behind the teeth it had pushed through. The sound it made—wet meat moving in a broken mouth. Ran fingers along the rope burns, checking the angle, the depth. The running bowline had left a specific pattern. Slipped sideways meant consciousness lasted longer. The priest made notes. Another data point in their study of how boys break.

He sniffed at the oil on the skin and his mouth pulled down. Said the kitchen grease wouldn't sanctify. Wrong kind for temple business. The goddess would refuse him. Mountain fire, not proper cremation. No rites. No gathering of ashes for family urns. Just disposal with the week's other failures.

Thrasybulos arrived while they stripped the body. His walking stick—carved from the scaffold that had held Nikias—clicked on stone as he circled the table. Studied Kyrillos like reading a completed equation. All those marks on tablets over the years, tracking which boys heard death in prophecy and which could function through it. Kyrillos had just provided the final data point.

He asked about signs. Had the boy shown acceleration of symptoms. Increased touching of the throat. More practice of the prophetic sounds.

I told him about our conversation. The promise to cut him down. The practice sounds. The way he'd said he wasn't real anymore. The torn fingertips from the lye. The constant measuring of beams.

Thrasybulos said prophecies were like seeds. Plant them in the right soil and they grow exactly as expected. The oracle hadn't predicted Kyrillos's death—just shown him the shape it would take. Given him the sounds to practice. Everything after was just watching the seed grow into what it was always going to become.

He asked if I'd heard the sounds when the body dropped.

I said yes. Three wet consonants. Exactly as the oracle had demonstrated.

He made deeper marks in his tablet. Said the mantis had been worth his price then. Accurate prophecies created accurate outcomes. Boys who couldn't empty themselves needed direction for their disposal. The oracle had provided that direction. Efficient.

The priest started his work. Shaved the head first, collected the hair for lesser rites. Pried out the teeth—twenty-eight, with four already missing from older violence. The teeth went into a bronze bowl, counted and recorded. Everything had to be inventoried, even the parts of broken boys.

They drained the blood but it came out dark, congealed. Not useful for proper ceremony. Still, it would mark thresholds in the support buildings, seal curses on behalf of paying clients. The compound wasted nothing, not even the blood of boys who'd killed themselves wrong.

The priest cut out the tongue—swollen and purple, tooth marks deep in the meat. Said he'd never seen one bitten through so completely. Usually they just chewed the edges. This one had gone all the way through in two places. The pain must have been extraordinary. But that was the body fighting the mind's decision. Everything about strangulation was the meat saying no while the will said yes.

We carried what remained to the mountain slope where failures burned. No ceremony. No gathering of boys to watch. Just inventory transfer. Other bodies waited—worn-out helot, infant from the women's quarters, another suicide who'd opened his wrists in the bath. They stacked Kyrillos on top.

The priest spoke inventory words, recording what was being returned to the mountain. Four bodies. Approximate weight. Cause of death. Expected burn time. All of it scratched into tablets like grain calculations.

The fire took him quick, kitchen grease making flames burn blue-green before settling to normal orange. Wrong color for funeral fire. Should have been the clean gold of proper oils. Instead, he burned like bad meat, like something that had spoiled before its time. The smell of rancid fat and overcooked pork carried on morning wind.

I stayed until bone showed through split flesh. Watched him become what we all became—smoke rising toward peaks where oracles breathed prophecy through other people's futures. The same mountains that had shown him his death now took back what remained.

That night in quarters, I burned his note. He heard me. Meaning the oracle had heard him practice those sounds. Had confirmed he was getting them right. All those nights pressing his throat, rehearsing the exact noise of strangulation. The oracle had been his audience, his validation that he understood his own ending perfectly.

The empty space at Kyrillos's station filled within days. Smaller boy, younger, transferred from another facility after freezing during first blood. I watched him explore the kitchen, learn the routines, count the roof beams with his eyes. His fingers were still intact. The lye hadn't started its work yet. Give it time. Give it a few months of scrubbing while real boys learned real violence. See how long before he started measuring drops and practicing sounds.

They all did that—looked up at doorways, calculated heights, tested loads. The compound produced two types of boys: the ones who went to Provincial work and the ones who went to rope. Sometimes you could tell which was which by how they entered rooms. The ones marked for hanging always looked up first.

The new boy asked about his predecessor on the third day.

I told him Kyrillos had been transferred.

He nodded but kept looking at those beams. He'd heard the truth in how I'd said it. Transferred to smoke, transferred to ash, transferred to the place where boys who couldn't empty themselves eventually went. The compound had tried to break Kyrillos down for their purposes, but the oracle had gotten there first, left him with nothing except those three sounds and the certainty of rope.

My advanced training accelerated after that. Languages, poisons, the patience needed for long-term placement. They were preparing me for Athens, though I didn't know it yet. While kitchen boys counted beams, I studied Persian verb forms and practiced drinking wine cut with water like democrats did. Different kinds of distance from different kinds of ending.

But sometimes in the armory, selecting bronze for the day's work, I'd remember Kyrillos's hands in that wash basin. Pink meat where fingertips should be. Steady motion that kept other movements at bay. The way he'd said he used to be good at finding the right angle for sharpening, back when he was real.

He'd been wrong about the dancing. The marks in the dust showed that. Just desperate scrambling for purchase that wasn't there, the meat's last argument with what the mind had decided. But he'd been right about those three sounds. When I cut him down, the severed rope released the pressure on his windpipe. Air rushed through the collapsed passages, made exactly those three wet consonants the oracle had taught him. His body speaking the prophecy one last time, confirming what he'd spent two years practicing.

The compound had two products: weapons and waste. I was being honed into a weapon sharp enough for Athens. Kyrillos had become waste the moment the oracle spoke. The only question had been how long his body would take to catch up with what his mind already knew.

I'd kept my promise. Cut him down like he'd asked. Kept him from becoming a morning lesson in what happened to boys who couldn't carry what the compound poured into them. The kitchen grease couldn't sanctify his suicide, but at least he hadn't swung there until count, hadn't become another demonstration of failure for boys who were still deciding which way they'd break.

The compound and the oracle had been competing to see who could empty him first. The oracle won by showing him his future so clearly he couldn't imagine any other. After that, every beam was the beam, every rope was the rope, every breath was practice for the moment breathing would stop.

He'd asked me to cut him down because even broken tools deserve that much. To disappear clean instead of becoming education for the next batch. I'd given him that.

It wasn't brotherhood—they'd removed that years ago. Just one broken boy doing inventory on another. Just a blood-bond fulfilling its purpose: ensuring that when one tool failed, the other would be there to process the disposal.

The scar on my palm ached for days after. Not guilt— that had been beaten out years ago. Just the body remembering it had been bound to something now gone. Even our scars were inventory systems, marking connections to tools no longer in service.

Clean cut. Clean burn. Clean ledger.

The compound's arithmetic, perfectly balanced.

CHAPTER 16

THE BURNING

THE DRUNK PRIEST dropped the oil twice before his apprentice took over. His brain was already going to vinegar and his hands shook unless they held bronze or wine. But his hands knew their business. When he found Kyrillos's forehead, his thumb moved in the exact pattern it had traced on a thousand dead boys. Practice making permanent what consciousness had dissolved.

They burned Kyrillos wrong on purpose. Everything about that morning was arranged—the bad wood, the rancid grease, even Melos's mockery. Another test disguised as routine.

They'd stacked him on top of a helot who'd coughed out his lungs and an infant from the women's quarters. Green wood mixed with dry. Bodies crossed wrong. Kitchen boys had built the pyre under supervision, following exact instructions to make it burn ugly and long. Make us stand there breathing lessons about what the compound did with broken tools.

When fire caught, the kitchen grease made Kyrillos burn blue-green like diseased meat. Should have been gold from proper oils. Should have been fast. Instead, we watched skin bubble and split while that rancid pork fat made everything wrong.

Twenty-three of us in formation, standing where we'd been told. The placement mattered—Thrasybulos had arranged us by some pattern I wouldn't understand for years. Put the ones who'd freeze next to ones who'd act. Put me where I could see both Melos and the shadows between buildings.

Melos spat when Kyrillos's belly split. The sound carried in morning stillness. He said dancing lessons finally worked out for someone. Got laughs from boys who needed to laugh at something.

I saw Thrasybulos in those shadows, that bone amulet moving between his fingers like he was counting. Not hiding—positioned. His stylus scratched wax with each boy who laughed, who stayed silent, who looked away. Later I'd understand he wasn't recording our reactions. He was confirming predictions made months ago about which tools would break which ways.

The fire worked through flesh, making architecture of what had been my blood-brother. Each rib emerging as fat rendered away. I counted them appearing—one, two, three—while inside my head I was already measuring mushroom doses. Not from loyalty to Kyrillos. From the mechanical need to balance an equation that Melos had made uneven.

When the corpse-gas made Kyrillos jerk and sigh, Melos went down on his ass. The laughter turned on him then —compound humor finding its level. He scrambled up, face red under the dirt, looking for someone to blame. Found me counting ribs instead of laughing.

He asked if I'd cut him down fast enough. If I was sweet on him. If I liked them warm.

That last one made the formation go quiet. Blood bonds were real as bronze. Suggesting that kind of violation crossed lines even we respected.

I looked at him once. Catalogued what mattered—the scar through his lip, how he held his weight, which leg he favored. Then back to counting ribs. Four visible now. Five. The meat pulling away from bone as moisture cooked out.

In the shadows, Thrasybulos made another mark.

That evening, I ground the mushrooms while thinking about the Egyptian's lessons. Amanita phalloides—the death cap. Slow enough to let them understand what was happening. Painful enough to be educational. Four days of organs liquefying while everyone watched another boy discover his mistake.

Melos started screaming about ropes and dancing by midnight. By morning, blood from both ends. The compound watched him die like they'd watched Kyrillos burn—as confirmation of patterns already recognized. When they burned Melos with the week's failures, nobody made jokes.

The whetstone sang against bronze. Perfect pitch when the angle was right. Tomorrow would bring new bodies, new problems, new boys discovering which side of excess they'd fall on.

But tonight I cleaned my blade and thought about Kyrillos asking me to cut him down. About keeping promises to the dead. About the exact amount of caring that kept you human without making you weak.

The compound had burned that lesson into us with kitchen grease and bad wood. Some boys learned it. Some became it.

The rest burned with their failures, making smoke that taught the same lesson to the next batch.

CHAPTER 17

THE SPIDER'S TEST

AGE 15

THRASYBULOS MADE us sit in a circle on stones so cold they pulled heat through our asses. Twenty-three of us, watching him work that bone amulet between his fingers —human knuckle worn smooth by decades of nervous handling. His bad leg stretched out, the old break from Mantinea that never healed right making him shift position every few minutes.

He said we'd been taught to observe. Tonight we'd learn the difference between seeing and understanding.

He pointed his walking stick at Dimitri. Told him to describe Marcus.

Dimitri gave the obvious shit. Six feet. Scar through left eyebrow. Favors right hand for blade work. Sleeps on his left side.

Thrasybulos's stick cracked against stone. Not Dimitri— just the granite beside him. Warning shot. He said a butcher's apprentice could see that much. Try again. This time, tell me why.

Dimitri tried harder. Marcus hoards bread despite getting regular rations for two years. Three spots—behind the loose stone, in his left sandal, sewn into his tunic hem. Still touches his ribs where they were broken during pankration. Breathes shallow on cold mornings because the bones set wrong.

Better. But still just observation. When Theron's turn came, something shifted.

Theron said Nikos has seven food caches. Not from hunger—we get enough now. From the memory of hunger. When anxious, he touches his ribs where Philippos broke them, but only when Philippos is in sight. Associates the pain with the person. Been sick twice this month, chest infection from sleeping near the mold corner. Buying poppy extract from Demetrios for the pain.

Everyone watched Nikos's hand twitch toward his ribs. Stop. Exactly where Theron had predicted.

Theron continued. Nikos knows Demetrios is selling medical supplies. Won't report it because he needs the medicine. But the moment his chest heals, he'll report Demetrios to curry favor with instructors. Already planning it. You can see it in how he looks at Demetrios—calculating when to spend that information.

The silence was complete. We'd all been watching each other for years, cataloging weapons and weaknesses. But

Theron saw the mechanisms. Not just what people did but why, and what they'd do next.

Thrasybulos almost smiled—would have been less terrifying if he had. He said good. Theron sees patterns. Now show me you understand perspective.

The real test started then. Not just observing but seeing through another's eyes. Most boys' brains locked when asked to make that shift.

He told me to describe how Thrasybulos himself saw me.

I studied him studying me. Saw myself reflected in his evaluation—not my self-image but his assessment of my use.

I said he sees me as a violence specialist. Can read a fight before it starts, know who'll die and how. Useful but limited. I only see people as potential violence—their capacity to deal or receive damage. Love, loyalty, family connections—those are invisible to me. Just background noise between violent potentials.

His stylus scratched wax, confirming.

I continued. He thinks I'll last twenty years doing Provincial work. Excellent at reading threats, removing problems. But I'll die in twenty minutes trying to infiltrate Athens because I move like a killer even when trying not to. Can't hide what I am because I can't see myself the way non-killers would see me. My blindness to normal human connection makes me perfect for certain work, useless for other kinds.

The scratching of his stylus on wax told me I'd hit it. Most boys couldn't make that jump—from seeing themselves to seeing how others saw them. Requires accepting you're not a person but a tool with specific limitations.

Theron had to describe how the instructors saw him.

He said they see me as useful but distasteful. Like a blade that cuts sideways. They need my ability to see connections, to manipulate through patience rather than force. But they despise how I survive through scheming instead of strength. The other boys need me to manage distributions, resolve conflicts. But they'd feed me to wolves the moment I wasn't useful. I'm a corruption of what they're trying to build—survival without honor.

More stylus scratching. Thrasybulos was sorting us in real time.

Some boys couldn't do it at all. They could list what they saw but couldn't model another mind seeing them. Those boys would stay in direct violence work—no subtlety required.

Others could do it partially. See through one perspective but not adjust for different viewers. They'd become Provincial workers like me—good at specific tasks within limitations.

But a few—Theron, two others—could shift perspectives like changing clothes. See through instructor eyes, citizen eyes, helot eyes. Understand how each would read them differently. Those boys vanished into intelligence work within days.

When Philippos had to describe how his own brother saw him, he broke. Started listing physical features, couldn't make the perspective jump. His brother was in the agoge, the real Spartan training. How would a citizen-in-training see his compound-rat brother?

He couldn't do it. Couldn't model a mind that saw him as shameful necessity. The compound taught us we were tools, but some boys still thought they were people. That delusion would sort them into work where it didn't matter.

By the end, Thrasybulos had his real answer. Not from what we'd said but from who could say it. The ability to see yourself through hostile eyes, to understand exactly how others calculated your worth—that was rarer than violence skill.

Within days, the intelligence-track boys were gone. Pulled for training in archives, languages, long-term thinking. The rest of us continued toward Provincial work, where reading violence patterns was enough.

That night, cleaning my blade in the lamplight, I understood what I'd admitted. That I could only see people as potential violence—their capacity to give or receive damage. Everything else was invisible. Love looked like weakness. Loyalty looked like exploitable patterns. Family looked like leverage points.

Thrasybulos had spent one evening confirming our limitations. I was perfectly broken—a tool so specialized for reading violence that I couldn't see anything else. In

Provincial work, that focus was strength. In Athens, it would have killed me in days.

But they'd pour Athens into me later, empty out the violence-reader and replace him with something that could smile at symposia. The Spider's Test had shown them exactly what needed breaking and what could stay.

I see people as violence problems requiring solutions. Theron saw them as networks to manipulate. Others saw different patterns or no patterns at all. The compound had broken us all differently, creating a toolkit of specialized damage.

That's what the Spider's Test really measured. Not intelligence but the specific shape of our blindness. What we couldn't see determined what we'd become.

CHAPTER 18

THE PIT

THE HOLDING pen stank of old piss and fear-sweat. Through the floor grate: impacts, choking, Thracian begging turning wet.

Fifteen of us pressed against the walls.

The door opened. Guards dragged Leandros up—face rearranged, fingers bent wrong, breathing wet through ruined teeth. They dumped him in the corner and studied us with the same measuring look we gave helots before harvest work.

My legs shook when they called us at noon. Not fear—the body knowing something was coming it couldn't prepare for.

The pit: fifteen paces across, walls too smooth to climb. Half-lit by design—pools of shadow to test who could function blind. Above us, viewing galleries packed with ephors, Thrasybulos with his tablets, citizens come to see their investment.

Five prisoners waited in the center. Not just criminals—killers who'd survived their own crucibles. The biggest had spiral tattoos and filed teeth. He spat near my feet, called us boy-fuckers in broken Greek. These men were reading us, cataloging weakness.

We spread along the walls. Make them come to us. But they waited, patient as predators.

The tattooed one pointed at Dimitri. When Dimitri didn't move, the smallest charged—something between spider and wolf, using shadows to fracture his approach. He got Dimitri's head in both hands, smashed it against stone twice. Then, when Dimitri went limp, thumbs into the eyes. Practiced work, finding exactly what would shut down more than sight.

Dimitri's scream changed pitch. Body rigid, then loose. Still breathing but already dead.

The small man wiped his thumbs clean. No celebration. Just work completed.

I understood then—this wasn't about combat. This was measuring who could think while drowning in violence.

The tattooed one started killing torches. Each dead flame eating more of the room.

Last torch out. Complete black.

In darkness, everything changed. Direction gone. My own breathing sounded foreign. Hands found my throat —big, calloused. I bit the thumb web where Damon had shown us the nerve cluster. Blood filled my mouth. The hands released.

I crawled left, hit something soft—a body. Kept moving.

Found a leg. The owner kicked my ribs. I held on, got my teeth on the Achilles tendon. Bit through. The tendon parted with a sound like rope snapping. I cataloged the anatomy while chewing—gastrocnemius separating from soleus, tissue cooling in my mouth. No revulsion. Just technical analysis. The pit hadn't changed us. It had revealed what we'd already become.

When torches flared from above, three of us stood among the wreckage. Theron against the wall, systematic knee-work on the man at his feet. Nikos with tissue in his teeth, not human anymore but appetite in boy-shape.

The tattooed one charged Theron. They went down hard, but Theron had already found the eyes—not gouging but pressing exactly where Dionysios had mapped the nerves. The Scythian's scream climbed, then stopped.

Three boys standing. None of them.

Pausanias descended, examined Dimitri's corpse with professional interest. Made a sound—disappointment or satisfaction, impossible to tell. He left without speaking. We were tools. You don't converse with hammers.

In the holding pen, the others pressed against the far wall, desperate to keep distance from what we'd become. A helot brought water but couldn't stop his hands shaking.

He'd lived around boys training to be killers for years, but we were different now. The pit had revealed us as function wrapped in flesh, and every instinct in his body knew it.

That night the compound gave us nothing. Let the lesson settle into our bones.

Three of us climbed out of that pit. Theron would die in Athens, throat opened by someone whose grandfather he'd sold. Nikos caught a spear in Syracuse. I survived to write this, which means the pit sorted correctly. Found the boy who could bite through tendons while cataloging anatomy.

The pit didn't make us killers. We already were. It just revealed how completely.

CHAPTER 19

THE WINNOWING

AGE 17

LYSANDER LOCKED fifteen of us in that stone box and told us seven could leave when light touched the western wall. The rest would feed the crows or take support duty. Simple. Except he didn't tell us how to become seven from fifteen. That was for us to solve while bleeding.

The drunk priest dropped three tags before his apprentice took over. His brain was vinegar now, hands remembering rituals his mind had dissolved. Called me Alexios, then Dimitri, then just boy. When he tried the blessing, wine-spit hit my cheek. I let it dry there. Moving meant notice.

The guards gave us knives. Good bronze. Nothing else.

When light touches the western wall's base, seven may leave. The bell grants mercy. Touch the marked ones at your peril.

The door slammed. Iron on stone.

The room stank immediately. Fear-sweat mixed with piss from boys whose bladders gave up at the door slam. Stone box cut so deep the walls wept constant. Everything calculated to break us in specific ways.

Thirteen oil lamps in wall niches. One already guttering.

We spread to walls without talking. I took a corner where stone met stone. Cold came through my tunic immediately. Could see the room, the door, the bronze bell hanging beside it.

I started counting. Fifteen boys. Fifteen tags. Seven could leave. But the math wasn't simple. Did we need one tag each? Two? What about the spare tags?

Some boys studied each other's tags. Three had notches filed into edges. Two had holes drilled through. One was different bronze—darker, older. The marked ones at your peril. But marked for what?

Kleinias broke first. Small boy, chest making wet sounds with each breath. He looked at the arithmetic that didn't favor him.

He walked to the bell. Rang it.

The sound came out wrong—crystalline, not bronze.

Two guards entered, spears leveled. One made a gesture —hand out, demanding his tag. Kleinias pulled it over his head. The guard shook his head, pointed back at us.

Understanding crawled across Kleinias's face. He had to give it to someone.

His eyes found Demetrios. They'd shared rations during the second winter. Kleinias handed him his tag.

The guards took him out. Door slammed again.

Fourteen of us now. Demetrios had two tags.

I understood. Seven boys could leave, but not necessarily with one tag each. If everyone needed two tags, seven boys would need fourteen total. One spare. But if some needed three? And those marked tags—were they worth different amounts?

Simon walked to the bell next. The oracle had told him water would take him. He rang. Same crystal sound. Same ritual.

Simon's eyes found me. We'd worked Gythium together. He took a step toward me, then stopped. Looked at my corner position, how I held my knife. Changed direction. Gave his tag to Marcus— younger, softer, someone who needed mercy more than I did.

My bladder released then. Hot piss down my leg. I didn't move. Just stood in my own waste while the count changed. Thirteen of us. Two boys with two tags. Eleven with one.

Thaddeus had a notched tag. I watched him fingering the grooves, trying to reach boys with unmarked tags. Nobody wanted to risk a marked tag without knowing what it meant.

That's when Solon moved. Big farm boy. Went for

Agathon slumped against the wall—eyes closed, body loose. Easy tag.

Solon reached. Agathon's blade went up under his arm, found the subclavian artery. Blood came in spurts—bright red, arterial.

Solon's face showed surprise. He'd survived the mountain march, the breaking ground, years of grinding. Now dying because he'd misread stillness for weakness.

He dropped. Tried to crawl toward the bell. I counted his breaths. At seventy the spurting stopped.

Nikos worked Solon's tag free. Two tags now.

The violence started then.

Three boys rushed Alexios in his corner. Two unmarked tags, one had drilled. Working together. So marked tags weren't instant death—just another variable.

Alexios got his blade into one's throat but missed the vessels. That boy kept fighting with his throat opened, making sounds I'd never heard—air through wrong pipes.

The other two got inside his guard. One hooked his arm. The second boy's knee came up. Temple strike. I heard bone crack—small sound like stepping on an egg.

Alexios dropped. His eyes stayed open but wrong. He tried to rise. Said clear as morning prayer that the goats were in the kitchen again.

Nothing else. Some memory knocked loose by the impact. Boot heel to jaw ended it.

I stayed in my corner, counting. Demetrios with two tags. Marcus with two. Nikos with two. Boys dying for arithmetic, not curses.

Castor rang the bell. Oracle-touched like Kyrillos had been. He understood the math.

His eyes found me. We'd trained poisons together. He walked over and pulled off his tag. The leather was warm, slick with fear-sweat.

He told me not to waste it.

Then gone. Four had chosen the bell. Eleven of us left. The bell wasn't mercy. It was another kind of selection. Who would sacrifice themselves? Who could inspire that sacrifice?

Philippos and another boy crashed together in the center. Both needed that second tag. They rolled through Solon's blood. The stones had drainage channels cut decades ago for exactly this purpose.

Philippos got on top. Started hitting. Grabbed the boy's throat. At thirty-two breaths, something gave way. He took the tag.

My legs shook from standing so long. The piss had gone cold against my skin. But moving from the corner meant becoming prey. The real test—not who was strongest, but who could endure the waiting.

I noticed the pattern in marked tags. Three notched, two drilled, one different bronze. Six marked tags total. Information that might matter.

The boy with different bronze tried to pry open the door. Guards heard. Door opened inward, fast. Spear took him through the chest. They dragged him out, left his bronze tag on the floor.

Nobody touched that abandoned tag.

Thaddeus with his notched tag made a run for the bell. Nikos intercepted him—already had two tags but always had to prove something. They crashed into the wall.

Thaddeus tried to bargain. Said he'd give his tag freely. Nikos got position. The blade went in under the jaw, found the brain stem. Thaddeus stopped mid-word.

Nikos took the tag. Three now. Wasteful.

Everyone exhausted now. I watched boys' shoulders shake from the effort of staying ready. That sour smell when muscles burn their own tissue for fuel.

The boy with the last notched tag rang the bell. Gave it to someone who already had a drilled tag. Nine of us left. The arithmetic was clear now.

The boy with just a drilled tag dove for the abandoned bronze. Another boy went for it too. They fought over that cursed tag like winter bread.

But they'd forgotten about me.

I left my corner for the first time. Legs barely worked—hours of standing still. Every joint screamed. But I'd waited for exactly this moment.

Got my blade into the first one's kidney. The other looked up as my knee found his nose. Cartilage crunched.

I took the tag. Three now. Enough to guarantee survival. Hours of watching, calculating, enduring my own waste —all for ten seconds of necessary violence.

The dying boys rang out in sequence. Strengthened those who'd already survived.

Seven of us left when light touched the western wall. Gray seepage under the door, then spreading across gore-painted stone.

Guards counted us. Counted tags. I had three. Nikos had three. The rest had two each. The marks hadn't mattered —just variables to track our decision-making.

Thrasybulos arrived. His walking stick clicked through blood puddles as he checked corpses against predictions. Another harvest complete.

That night, washing blood from my knife, I understood. The compound hadn't tested combat—we'd proven that in the pit. They wanted to see who could calculate while drowning in violence. Who could track multiple variables while standing in their own piss. Who could endure hours of tension then act decisively.

Seven of us survived by becoming what the compound needed. Not the strongest—I'd stood in my corner most of the night. Not the fastest—I'd moved exactly twice. But the ones who could read the arithmetic of survival and solve for X while other boys solved for blood.

The winnowing had worked exactly as designed. Fifteen boys became seven tools, with wastage calculated and channels cut to drain it.

Simple arithmetic. Everything else was just the method.

CHAPTER 20
THE ASSIGNMENT
AGE 17

ALKETES MOVED like meat hung wrong. Twenty years of Provincial work had left him with a permanent list to the left—kidney wound that never healed right, he'd tell us later. Made him walk like he was always compensating for weight that wasn't there. His right hand was missing the last two fingers, bitten off at the second knuckle. Clean scars, old work. Said a helot woman had taken them while he was taking her son. Fair trade, he'd called it, though he'd opened her throat after.

We met him in the eastern courtyard three days after the winnowing. My knife still had blood worked into the cord wrapping—some of it mine, most of it not. Marcus kept touching his ribs where they'd never healed right since the meat circle—the winnowing had found that old weakness. Philippos breathed through his mouth, nose still swollen shut. We stood in morning shadow while frost melted off the stones, trying not to show how much everything hurt.

Alketes squatted despite his bad kidney—the movement made him wince but he did it anyway. Pulled out a stick, started drawing in the dirt between the drainage channels. Three circles. Potter. Wife. Son.

He told us the potter ran the only workshop between here and Therapne. Asked when the village would notice if he died tonight.

His voice came out damaged, like he'd screamed too long once and never got it all back. I counted seventeen breaths between question and Marcus stepping forward. Marcus, eager to show he'd earned his winnowing tag despite the boot-prints still purple on his ribs.

Behind us, Nikos shifted his weight, hand moving unconsciously to his left hip where I knew he kept emergency rations sewn into the tunic seam. Still checking his caches even though Provincial boys got fed regular. Some habits carved too deep to break.

Said tomorrow, when the workshop didn't open.

Alketes's stick cracked across Marcus's knuckles. Not hard —Provincial men learned economy in everything—but sharp enough to split skin. Marcus's blood spotted the dirt next to the circles. Said wrong. Told Marcus to try again.

I watched how Alketes held the stick. Three fingers on his maimed hand, thumb and middle finger making a strange grip. He'd adapted. Everything about him showed adaptation—the way he squatted despite the kidney, how he'd turned his body to keep his good ear toward us. Left ear was just a hole, the shell carved away neat. Professional work.

I said three days, when orders weren't filled.

Still wrong. He drew lines between the circles, and I noticed his remaining fingers had burn scars across the tips. Old interrogation work, probably. The kind where you need to handle hot metal regularly.

Said the wife, Melia, was a better potter than him. She'd find him dead tonight, have the workshop running by dawn. Maybe send his body to the hills, maybe dump him in the ravine. Either way, the workshop keeps functioning.

Marcus rubbed his split knuckles. Blood had gotten into the creases—I knew from experience that would take days to wash out. Said so we kill her too.

Alketes asked when. The morning sun had climbed enough to hit the courtyard wall behind us. I felt it on my neck, that first warmth after three days in the winnowing room's cold. My body wanted to turn toward it like a plant, but movement meant attention.

Same night?

Another crack of the stick. This time across Marcus's shins. Said six apprentices with no master means panic. They run to the headman. Headman sends riders to Sparta. Investigation. The territory goes nervous. Productivity drops for months.

He added more circles. The apprentices. His stick moved wrong in that three-fingered grip, but precise. Each circle exactly the same size. Provincial work taught that kind of consistency—every cut the same depth, every approach the same patience.

Said she'd been teaching them. Spreading the knowledge he kept tight. One man, one workshop, one throat to cut. Now it's seven people who can throw pots. Seven potential problems.

I counted the circles. Calculated the timeline. Six months to neutralize a workshop. Maybe eight. My mind was already running the economics—lost productivity, investigation costs, the price of fear spreading through the territories. All from questions a six-year-old asked.

I began to see it. Said kill her first. Make it look like sickness. The apprentices need her, but they know enough to keep working. They'll fight over who takes control.

He said better. Asked when.

Two months. Long enough that it seems unconnected.

Behind us, someone's stomach growled. We'd had nothing since before the winnowing. Three days on water and whatever strength we'd stored. Alketes heard it, smiled with half his mouth. The other half didn't move—nerve damage from whatever took his ear.

He drew an X through her circle. Then tapped the son. Said this was Alexios. Soft hands, never worked clay. But learning numbers. Could track inventory, handle accounts. Dangerous combination—craft knowledge in the mother, business knowledge in the son.

Marcus suggested accident. His voice came out thick— the split lip from yesterday hadn't healed. Made certain consonants whistle. Kiln explosion. He's clumsy.

When?

Two months after the mother.

Alketes nodded. That half-smile again. Drew an X through the son. Circled the potter three times. The stick left grooves in the dirt deep enough to last until rain. Said now he's alone. No wife. No heir. Drinking. Making mistakes. Six months later?

I said suicide. Hangs himself from a workshop beam. Everyone saw it coming.

The word 'hangs' made me think of Kyrillos. Two years dead now, but I could still see the grooves his feet had left in the storage room dust. The compound recycled every-thing, even death methods.

He asked about the apprentices.

They divide the workshop. None strong enough to dominate. Power disperses.

He erased the circles with his boot, started over. The movement made him shift weight off his bad side. This time, a smaller circle in the center. Said but we're not here for the potter.

From his satchel—leather so old it had gone black, Provincial issue from before we were born—he pulled a wax tablet. On it, a child's drawing. Stick figures under a sun. The wax was fresh, probably carved this morning for this lesson. Said this was the potter's nephew. Six years old. Smart little fuck who asked questions. Why do we work for them? Why do they take our grain? Where does it go?

The other boys leaned in. Nikos had joined us—I hadn't heard him approach. Ten years of compound training made us all ghosts, but Provincial men like Alketes were something else. They'd learned to move through the world like smoke, leaving nothing behind but perfectly timed deaths.

He said questions spread through children like sickness. They repeat them. Parents hear. Start thinking. So we remove the questioning child. But—his stick stabbed the dirt hard enough to snap the tip—kill a child, you make a martyr. Parents rage. Communities unite through grief. Instead?

He drew new patterns. House. Workshop. Trail between. His fingers might have been ruined but they knew their business. Each line exact despite the missing digits.

Said the boy goes missing. We leave signs—struggle, blood trail to the potter's workshop. Under the kiln, we plant evidence. Small bones. Not just his. Evidence of others.

I saw it complete now. The timeline, the investigation, the community response. All of it cascading from one child's questions. Said they think the potter killed his own nephew.

And others. The community tears itself apart. Who knew? Who protected him? The woman must have helped—always in the workshop. The son kept books, must have noticed children disappearing.

Marcus breathed that the village kills them for us. Blood had dried on his chin from the split lip. Made him look younger somehow, like a child who'd fallen playing.

Enthusiastically. Burns the workshop. Salts the earth. The apprentices scatter, terrified of association. We've removed not just three problems but the entire structure. And the beautiful part—

He stood, and I heard his knee pop. That wet sound joints make when they've been broken and healed wrong. Dusted his hands on his tunic. The dust stuck to the burn scars.

Said they thank us for revealing the monster. Increase their loyalty. Their productivity. Their gratitude that Sparta protects them from such evil.

The silence stretched. Not from horror—we'd seen worse. Three days ago I'd stood in my own piss while boys died around me. But from understanding. This wasn't about killing. This was about engineering human behavior through precise application of violence.

Philippos shifted, and I heard his broken ribs grinding. That small sound of bone on bone. We were all carrying our winnowing wounds, but Alketes had twenty years of Provincial damage written on his body. This was our future—fingers bitten off, organs that never healed right, moving through the world like broken animals who'd learned to function anyway.

He said tomorrow we go north. Three months in the territories. We'd learn to read villages like texts. Every removal is an edit that changes the meaning. Get it wrong, you strengthen what you meant to weaken. Get it right...

He left it unfinished. We understood.

That night, scraping dried blood from under my nails—it takes oil to get it all, and we had none—I studied his drawings in my mind. The circles. The connections. How one child's questions could topple a workshop, scatter a trade, terrify a region into deeper submission. All through knowing exactly where to apply pressure.

I counted the timeline again. Eight months from first death to final resolution. Thirty-two weeks. Two hundred and twenty-four days. All to silence a six-year-old who asked why.

The compound had taught us to kill. Alketes was teaching us to think. The scars on his body showed the price of that education—each missing piece a lesson learned, each wound a village properly edited.

Three months later, I could read a village in a day. Find its fracture points in an hour. Plan removals that looked like justice rather than terror.

The potter's nephew never existed. It was just a teaching tool. But somewhere in the territories, a real child was asking real questions. And now I knew exactly what to do about it.

By then, I'd have my own scars to match Alketes's. You can't edit human communities without them editing you back. But that morning in the courtyard, watching a three-fingered hand draw circles in the dirt, I thought Provincial work was just killing with better planning.

I'd learn different. We all would. Those of us who survived long enough.

CHAPTER 21

THE HARVEST TEST

AGE 18

THRASYBULOS GAVE me Gythium and a wool merchant's identity. Four months minimum. The port where I'd killed the tax collector with Kyrillos would now house me for a season.

He said I knew Gythium already. Now learn to live in it.

Two weeks later, I arrived sick from rough seas, playing Nikomenes of Corinth for a wool trader who thought I was exactly what I claimed. The port still stank of fish rot and tar. But now I had to live in it, not just pass through for a killing.

The boarding house near the docks teemed with exactly the people Thrasybulos wanted mapped. I shared a room with two longshoremen—Praxites who talked constantly and Demon who watched everything. First night, Demon studied me.

Said I moved different for a wool factor's boy.

My body had already betrayed me. I forced a laugh, made myself slouch. Said three older brothers. You learn to dodge or get beaten.

Week six, the guard from four years ago drank at my tavern. Same locked knee where Kyrillos had damaged it. Same story about compound boys. Said they moved different. That different walk they have.

Old training surfaced—shoulders squaring, weight shifting forward. I caught myself, forced a stumble, knocked over my cup. The wine spreading across rough wood while my pulse hammered. Not from fear. From the effort of being wrong.

Weeks passed in deliberate mediocrity. I learned wool grades, mapped intelligence networks, identified which merchants fed Athens information. But something else was happening.

Week twelve, something shifted. Menandros extended our stay and I felt... relief. Not because the mission continued. Because I didn't have to stop being Nikomenes.

His mediocre life fit perfectly. No checking shadows. No cataloging exits. Just wool grades and weak wine and conversations about nothing. I'd sit in taverns listening to dock workers complain about their wives and catch myself nodding along like I gave a shit about marriage problems.

Then Praxites noticed something. Said three months and

you never visit the brothels. Every young man from Corinth I've known can't wait to try Gythium girls.

A probe. Real wool factors' assistants would jump at whores. That night, they took me to a brothel that reeked of cheap perfume. Gave me a Thessalian girl, maybe sixteen, dead-eyed from the work. I paid her to talk while making fucking sounds through thin walls where Demon and Praxites listened.

The fake-fucking wasn't the performance. The performance was pretending I didn't prefer it to real intimacy. Easier to make rutting sounds than remember how actual connection felt.

Week sixteen, I submitted my final report. Complete intelligence map of Gythium's leaks. Next day, Provincial teams swept through. Five merchants arrested. Two resisters dead. Perfect surgical removal based on my intelligence.

After Provincial teams cleaned out my targets, I comforted Menandros while the port bled. He kept asking why them about his arrested friend.

I said maybe that was just his cover. Watched him process the idea that anyone could be anyone. Including me. Especially me.

I stayed two unnecessary weeks. Not for cover. To feel the hole I'd torn in the port's fabric. To watch it struggle to heal. To be the concerned assistant bringing soup to grieving widows whose husbands I'd marked for removal.

When I finally returned to the compound, only three of us had succeeded. Thrasybulos reviewed my reports.

Asked why I stayed too long after.

I told him I wanted to see the aftermath. How the network rebuilt itself.

But that was a lie I told us both. I wanted to see if I could still find my way back to myself after four months of being nobody. The answer sat cold in my chest.

He said Athens next. But Athens will take years, not months. Asked if I could be Nikias for decades.

I said I could be anyone.

And felt Aristarchus dissolve a little more, making room for whoever they'd need me to become next.

CHAPTER 22

THE ARITHMETIC

AGE 18

Six weeks I lived above a fulling shop in Tegea, learning to disappear into stench. The piss-reek covered everything—concentrated urine splashing into vats below, the acrid burn of it mixing with wet wool and lye until breathing meant tasting other men's waste. It soaked into my clothes, my hair, the bread I ate. By the third week, I'd stopped noticing it. By the sixth, I'd become it.

That's what Thrasybulos was really testing. Not whether I could kill a magistrate—any Provincial boy could open a throat. But whether I could marinate in someone else's life so completely that even I forgot what I really was.

The magistrate I'd come to kill was almost beside the point. Grain skimmer, selling garrison schedules to Athens. Standard corruption requiring standard removal. But Thrasybulos had been specific about method. Six weeks minimum surveillance. Live where no

Spartan would live. Eat what no citizen would eat. Become unremarkable through sheer endurance of the remarkable.

The fulling shop owner thought I was a merchant's son from Argos, recovering from fever. Weak story but it explained why I never left my room, why I paid in advance, why I looked gray as old meat. He'd check on me daily—worried I'd die and leave a corpse to explain. I'd make myself cough, complain about the smell, count coins with shaking hands. Performing weakness until weakness became truth.

From my window, I could see the magistrate's routine. Dawn prayers at the household shrine. Morning inspection of grain wagons. Afternoon receiving petitioners. Evening at his mistress's house—a weaver who lived three streets over. The patterns never varied. Men who steal think routine protects them. Really it just makes the killing easier to schedule.

But I wasn't watching him to plan his death. I was watching him to understand how a man lives when he thinks he's safe. How his shoulders sat when no threat registered. How he laughed with his mouth fully open. How he touched his purse without checking for watchers. These were the things I couldn't fake because I'd never felt them. Six weeks of observation to learn what safety looked like on a body.

The piss-stench was its own education. First day, I'd gagged with every breath. By the fifth day, I'd learned to breathe shallow through my mouth. By the tenth, my body had given up protesting. By the twentieth, I'd pour myself wine in that room and taste nothing but fullers' piss. The human body adapts to anything if you force it long enough.

Other tenants lived in the building. A Thessalian whore who worked the harbor. Two brothers from Argos, selling olive oil that was mostly pig fat. An old woman who talked to cats that had been dead for years. They'd nod when we passed on the stairs, our shared misery making us invisible to each other. Nobody looks too close at people living above piss-vats.

Week three, the magistrate's pattern changed. His son arrived from Corinth—soft-handed gambler who'd burned through his allowance. They'd argue in the street about money, the son's voice carrying wine-slur even at dawn. New variable to track. New patterns to learn. I watched them fight outside the grain warehouse, memorizing how fathers and sons wound each other with words.

Week four, I got sick. Not performance—actual fever from the fumes, the diet of bread and watered wine, the accumulated poison of living in my own cover. Spent three days shitting water, so weak I had to crawl to the piss-pot. The fulling shop owner brought me barley soup, told me I looked like death warming over. I thanked him in a voice I didn't recognize—hoarse, grateful, pathetic. Somewhere in that fever, Nikias began.

Week five, the magistrate's mistress left for Mantinea. Family emergency I'd arranged through forged letters. The magistrate would be alone on the fifth day after harvest, his son drunk at the symposium. Perfect timing I'd calculated from patterns observed through piss-fog and fever dreams.

Week six, I'd become the arithmetic of patience. Six weeks multiplied by seven days multiplied by the twenty-four hours I'd spent breathing pollution. The compound had taught me to count everything, but this was different. This was counting how long a boy could steep in another life before forgetting he was performing.

The night before the killing, I lay on my straw mattress—crawling with bugs, stained with six weeks of sweat—and tried to remember the compound. But it felt distant, like something I'd dreamed. What felt real was the piss-stench, the fever-weakness, the gray existence of a failed merchant's son. I had to check my knife to remember I was there to kill someone.

Fifth day after harvest. I waited in his mistress's room, but I waited different than I would have six weeks ago. Slouched instead of coiled. Breathing through my mouth from habit. When he entered with his son—the drunk demanding five hundred drachma—I almost forgot to stand properly. Almost stayed in character too long.

But muscle memory runs deeper than assumed identity. When the moment came, the knife found his throat with thirteen years of training behind it. His son pissed himself. I let him run. Made the magistrate write his confession. All standard Provincial work.

What wasn't standard was how I felt doing it. Distant. Like I was watching someone else kill through Nikias's eyes. The compound had taught me violence. Those six weeks had taught me to bury it so deep even I couldn't find it without effort.

All standard Provincial work.

Two days later, Thrasybulos summoned me. I still reeked of fullers' piss despite three river washes.

He said Alexias was compromised in Athens. Twenty years of cover blown by one old memory.

He asked if I could pretend to be Athenian for thirty years. Maybe more.

I said I could pretend to be anything.

He studied me. That recognition of a craftsman whose tool had exceeded specifications. When boys said they could pretend to be anything, they meant accents and customs. When I said it, we both knew I meant something else.

He said they'd pour Athens into me.

I thought about those six weeks above the piss-vats. How somewhere in the fever, I'd forgotten I was pretending. Athens would take longer. That was all.

That night, burning my clothes from Tegea, I understood. The magistrate's death had been incidental. The real test was those six weeks.

Any fool could kill. But could they disappear so completely that even they forgot what they were?

Six weeks of piss had proven I could.

CHAPTER 23

THE POURING

THEY GAVE me a dead man's name and told me to grow into it. Nikias of Acharnae, grain merchant's son, twenty years old. The real one had died of fever on the road to Corinth—no family left to contradict my existence. Thrasybulos handed me the forged documents like they were bronze, weighing exactly what a life should weigh.

I entered Athens with a carpenter's apprentice who stank of sawdust and sour wine. He thought I was running from debt in Megara. I paid him to forget he'd seen me, though he was too drunk to remember anyway. The gates were crowded with morning traffic—farmers bringing produce, merchants counting loads, democracy grinding forward on the backs of men who voted between harvests.

My body betrayed me immediately.

A drunk stumbled into me near the Kerameikos. My hand moved for his throat before I could stop it—thirteen years of training overriding conscious thought. Caught myself, turned it into steadying him instead. He mumbled thanks through wine-breath while my fingers trembled from aborting the strike. Every instinct screamed that his throat was exposed, that the crowd would cover the sound, that his death would mean nothing. I forced myself to pat his shoulder, ask if he was well. Democratic concern. Athenian softness. The exact kind of worthless kindness that marked Athenian citizens as prey.

The room I rented sat above a baker in the Skambonidai district. Cheap but not suspicious. The whole quarter reeked of fermented dough and the tannery runoff that flowed down from the Keramikos. Democracy had a smell—sweat and sewage and too many bodies pretending their votes made them equal. The baker's wife had questions—where was my family, what brought me to Athens, did I know anyone? I made myself stammer through answers. Mother dead. Father's business failed. Hoping to start fresh. The stuttering came hard—we'd been beaten for imperfect speech at the compound. Now I had to perform imperfection constantly.

That first night, I sat on a straw mattress that smelled of the previous tenant's sickness and practiced being wrong. How would Nikias hold a cup? Not balanced for throwing, fingers loose and careless. How would he walk? Not checking corners, not cataloging exits. Weight back on his heels like men who'd never run for their lives.

I spent hours relearning to move like someone who'd never been emptied. Like someone whose mother hadn't given him to the state at seven. Like someone who'd never stood in his own piss while boys died for arithmetic.

The hardest part was the talking. Athenians never shut up. They complained about prices, gossiped about neighbors, argued about fucking everything. Who was fucking whose wife. Whether the fishmonger was watering his garum. Which brothel had the cleanest girls. All those words pouring out like they cost nothing.

At the compound, silence was survival. Words were expensive, dangerous, counted. Here I had to spend them freely, stupidly, the way democrats did. Had to have opinions on shit that didn't matter. The new tribute. The harbor fees. Whether Kleon was a cunt or just acted like one.

I practiced in my room first, speaking to walls about nothing. The baker below probably thought I was mad. Mad was fine. Mad was better than what I actually was.

The agora nearly broke me that first month. Too many bodies pressed together, too many angles to watch. The place stank of rotting vegetables, incense from the god-botherers, and that particular smell of democratic sweat —men who thought arguing made them important. My hands kept finding knife positions when vendors grabbed my arm. Every crowded moment, my body wanted to create space, establish position, prepare for violence that wasn't coming.

One afternoon a sophist cornered me about the nature of identity. The only actual philosopher I met that year, drunk on his own importance and cheap wine. His breath reeked of onions and self-satisfaction. Was the self constant or changing? If a man replaced every thought and habit, was he still the same man?

I gave him the fumbling answers Nikias would give. But inside, I knew the answer. I was pouring myself out daily, replacing every trained response with its opposite. Soon there'd be nothing left of the compound's work. Just Nikias shaped like a man. Another successful investment by the state, another tool functioning exactly as designed.

The gymnasium was worse than the agora. Naked bodies wrestling, but wrong. No killing intent. They grappled for points, for honor, for applause. When a trainer corrected my stance—too aggressive, too ready—I had to apologize, laugh, claim I'd learned from rough country men. Then force myself to wrestle badly, leaving openings that made my teeth grind. Watching Athenians play at violence was like watching children play at war with wooden swords. They had no idea what their bodies were actually for.

But the worst was learning to sleep wrong.

Every night for thirteen years, I'd slept light as a bird, ready to wake at footsteps. Now I had to sleep like Athenians—deep, trusting, vulnerable. I'd force myself to lie with my back exposed, door unbarred. Wake myself when I'd automatically moved to a defensive position. Reset. Do it again.

Months of this. Unlearning everything that kept men alive, learning everything that made them soft.

I started keeping a drunk friend—Mikon, failed sculptor who'd drink with anyone who'd pay. He was perfect cover. His slurred philosophy, his grabbiness, his need to piss every hundred steps. Nobody looked twice at two young men stumbling through streets. Nobody noticed I was always sober, always watching, always calculating behind Nikias's empty smile. Cataloging pressure points in the democracy, marking which voting tribes could be turned with a few strategic removals.

The breakthrough came in a whorehouse near the port. Mikon had dragged me there, insisting Nikias needed to live a little. The girl they gave me was maybe sixteen, Thracian, with bruises on her arms from previous customers. She moved like someone expecting violence.

I paid her to talk instead. She was confused at first—customers usually had simpler needs. But loneliness loosened her tongue. She told me about her village, her brothers, how she'd ended up here. Stories that meant nothing to Nikias but everything to intelligence gathering.

That became my method. Pay whores to talk. They knew which merchants visited, which politicians had specific tastes, who was selling what information. All while maintaining Nikias's reputation as a soft boy who'd rather talk than fuck. The compound had taught me to extract information through bronze and pressure. Athens taught me that lonely people would give you everything for the price of attention.

By winter, I'd built a life. Rented a warehouse near the port. Hired two freedmen who thought I was an idiot overpaying for their labor. Started moving small amounts of grain, deliberately mismanaging enough to seem genuinely incompetent rather than suspiciously so.

The carpenter I'd entered with saw me in the agora one day. Didn't recognize me at first. When he did, he laughed, said I looked like a proper Athenian now. Fat and happy and stupid. I laughed too, bought him wine, let him tell everyone how the scared boy from Megara had made good.

But sometimes, cleaning my perfectly wrong blade in my perfectly wrong way, I'd remember the compound. Not with longing—that had been beaten out too. Just aware-ness of what I'd been before the pouring started. Like remembering a dream of someone else's life. Or like trying to remember my mother's face before that morning she woke me in darkness. Both memories belonged to someone who no longer existed.

By the second winter, visiting merchants started calling me Nikias the Soft, the grain dealer who'd overpay rather than haggle too hard. Perfect. Let them think that while I mapped their connections, their debts, their vulnerabili-ties. Every merchant who cheated me, every official who took bribes, every name they dropped while drunk—all of it cataloged, sorted, waiting to become leverage when the Thirty needed it.

Thirty-three years I'd hold this shape. Now, at fifty-three, writing this truth in my own warehouse while Athens burns outside, my hand still wants to move like Nikias would move it. Soft and careless and stupid.

The compound won completely. They'd made me empty enough to hold an entire false life without spilling a drop.

Or so I tell myself. But here's what I can't stop thinking about, here in my countinghouse with democratic blood funding my retirement: Sometimes my own children call me Father in that same trusting tone the magistrate's son used, and I have to leave the room. Sometimes I test myself—try to hold a blade the way I learned at seven, try to stand the way Marcus did before they beat it out of him, try to remember any of our names before they became numbers.

I can't. Even trying feels like betraying Nikias.

The compound didn't just make me empty enough to hold a false life. They made me prefer it. This soft merchant who overpays for grain and can't haggle—he never had to watch boys eat their own dead. Never had to choose between two tags or the bell. Never had to cut his blood-brother down from a kitchen beam.

Nikias is the better man. Even if he's built on democratic corpses. Even if he's hollow.

Maybe especially because he's hollow.

HISTORICAL NOTE

The Krypteia existed. Ancient sources confirm Sparta used boys as state terrorists to control the helot population through systematic murder. What they don't tell us is how children became killers. This novel fills that silence. While Aristarchus is fictional, his world is not—the helot ratios, the annual war declaration, the intelligence networks, the 1,500 Athenians killed by the Thirty. If anything, I may have understated the brutality.

GLOSSARY

Agoge - The official Spartan education system for citizens' sons

Drachma - Silver coin; standard currency in ancient Greece

Ephor - One of five elected Spartan magistrates with power over policy and kings

Helot - State-owned slaves, primarily from conquered Messenia

Hoplite - Heavy-armed Greek soldier who fought in formation

Krypteia - Secret force of young Spartans trained to kill helots

Lochos - Military unit in the Spartan army

Mantis - Prophet or seer who interprets divine will

Obol - Small silver coin; six obols equal one drachma

Pankration - "All-power" - ancient fighting style combining wrestling and striking

Perioikoi - Free non-citizens in Spartan territory who could own land but not vote

Phalanx - Dense military formation with overlapping shields

Plantanista - Training ground for the agoge, located between two rivers

Stade - Unit of distance, approximately 600 feet

Syssitia - Communal dining clubs where Spartan citizens ate together

Talent - Unit of weight, approximately 57 pounds

Trireme - Greek warship with three rows of oars

Xiphos - Short sword used by Greek warriors

OSIRIS MANDARIN PRESS

We publish speculative works that inhabit the spaces between fiction and scholarship. Our books take the form of fictional academic monographs, imagined institutional documents, and scholarly hoaxes that reveal more truth than conventional nonfiction.

From reconstructed memoirs of ancient state terrorism to symposia on concepts that don't yet exist, from leaked reports from impossible bureaucracies to academic papers from parallel universes—we create rigorous fictions that expand the boundaries of knowledge by acknowledging its limits.

Our authors approach the unwritten, the undocumented, and the unspeakable not as absences but as opportunities for disciplined imagination. They produce fictional primary sources, theoretical frameworks for nonexistent phenomena, and scholarly apparatus for impossible histories.

We publish books that could exist, examining what should be known, through forms that blur the line between discovery and invention.

For readers who understand that certain truths can only be told through elaborate lies.